Death

The American filled his glass and came back with it and said to Bishop:

"Well, I saw the firing-squad form up. They waited for the command. We all waited for that, I guess. I stood there trying to work out the morality of the thing, but of course I couldn't. Then it happened. I had to stop philosophizing pretty fast because the scene had changed. Most of it remained just about the same. It was frozen— *we* were frozen by our surprise. A second back, three blindfolded men had been standing against the wall. Now they were spreadeagled on the ground, dead. And I'd been watching, you understand? I hadn't been looking around, anywhere else. I watched them fall. They fell dead. They fell like stones. Without a sound...."

Also by Adam Hall

Knight Sinister
Queen in Danger
Bishop in Check
Pawn in Jeopardy

Published by
HarperPaperbacks

ADAM HALL
Rook's Gambit

original title *Dead Circuit*

HarperPaperbacks
A Division of HarperCollinsPublishers

This is a work of fiction. The characters, incidents, and dialogues are products of the author's imagination and are not to be construed as real. Any resemblance to actual events or persons, living or dead, is entirely coincidental.

HarperPaperbacks *A Division of* HarperCollins*Publishers*
10 East 53rd Street, New York, N.Y. 10022

Copyright © 1955 by Elleston Trevor
All rights reserved. No part of this book may be used or reproduced in any manner whatsoever without written permission of the publisher, except in the case of brief quotations embodied in critical articles and reviews. For information address HarperCollins*Publishers*, 10 East 53rd Street, New York, N.Y. 10022

This book was originally published under the title *Dead Circuit*.

Cover photography by Herman Estevez

First HarperPaperbacks printing: March 1991

Printed in the United States of America

HarperPaperbacks and colophon are trademarks of HarperCollins*Publishers*

10 9 8 7 6 5 4 3 2 1

*For Noël Hood
the B.B.C.'s inimitable Miss Gorringe*

1st MOVE

THE LIGHTS flicked to green. Bishop dropped the gears into mesh and edged the elegant sedanca through the pack of traffic, swinging left into King's Road. He said: "We lunch home, or we lunch out?"

Miss Gorringe turned the newspaper, folding it. Then she looked through her side-window.

"Where are we?"

Bishop glanced at her. "King's Road." Miss Gorringe had been born in King's Road, lived there now, and would probably die there if she weren't nimble across the Zebras. She was gazing through the side-window now as if she were driving down Prince's Street or Fifth Avenue, somewhere unfamiliar. Bishop said, "If we lunch out, it should be at the Bolero, and I'll turn back before we reach home. Alternatively

I could give you shock-treatment before your coma becomes permanent."

"I've just seen something in the paper." She went on gazing at the shops and traffic and people.

Bishop said, "By your expression, I can only think it was an article on self-hypnosis."

"No, it was the stop-press."

"Which says—?"

"They didn't hang Jones."

Bishop drove slowly between a bicycle and a suicidal road-sweeper. He said:

"They didn't what?"

"They didn't hang Jones."

"Who's Jones?"

Miss Gorringe lit a cocktail-cigarette and went on looking out of the window. She said, "He was a man convicted of murder and sentenced to death. The appointment was for nine o'clock this morning at Pentonville. But they couldn't hang him."

"Why not?"

"He died."

"What of?"

"They don't know."

"Where did he die?"

"In the death-cell."

"More suitable than in the living-room."

Miss Gorringe said, "That was in bad taste, Hugo."

His tone scarcely changed; it just had the edge off.

"Barbarism always leaves a bad taste. When we condemn a man to be hanged by the neck until he is dead, only a hypocrite can treat the matter with any reverence. When did this one die?"

"An hour before his time, at about eight o'clock. There's to be an early inquest."

Bishop said reasonably, "There always is, on a hanged man."

"I must remind you—Jones wasn't hanged. This inquest won't be the customary formality of confirming his neck was broken. They don't know what made this one die."

Bishop turned into Cheyne Mews. If Miss Gorringe had things on her mind, they could talk better at home than at the Bolero. He drew the car in past the yellow front-door and switched the engine off, and waited. In a moment Miss Gorringe said:

"You'll have to put off your trip to Luxembourg."

"I don't see."

"Just for a day or two, until we know whether this is interesting or not."

"You can find out, while I'm away. It's only for a few days."

"I might want you here. You might have to work quickly."

"You don't convince me."

"I'm trying to convince myself, but you don't give me thinking space. It's my job to find you material for your case-book; at least you could help."

He sat with his hands draped over the steering-wheel, and wondered if there were time for another pipe before lunch, and if Gorry would come out of her trance before evening. He sat there without moving or saying anything for five minutes; then she said:

"I know what it is."

He took his hands off the wheel and opened the door and said, "That's a relief. Now can we go and have something to eat?"

"Yes. They're sending up some scampi. Will that do?"

"Perfectly." They got out of the car. Half-way up the stairs, he said, "So you know what it is. What is it?"

"I'll dig out my files."

They went into the long, high-ceilinged room. The Princess Chu Yi-Hsin was on the davenport, watching them with half-closed amethyst eyes as Bishop dropped his gloves and Miss Gorringe went to her desk.

"They're sending up some scampi," Bishop said to the Siamese. She yawned luxuriously in his face. She didn't know what he had said, or she would have shot off the davenport and thrown herself at the service-lift. A cat has a phrase for scampi; it is Christmas-in-Paradise.

"Hugo."

"M'm?"

He wandered towards the desk where Miss Gorringe sat. She peeled off a newspaper-cutting and read from it:

" 'Three political prisoners fell dead in the execution yard of Madrid's smallest prison yesterday morning, a few minutes before the firing-squad was ready to shoot. The cause of death has been given officially as heart-failure.' "

Miss Gorringe looked up at Bishop. He said:

"That's just a filler—"

"Of course it's a filler. Six lines. That doesn't make it a story fabricated merely to fit the space. It's from the Channel Agency."

Bishop walked up and down. "Jones dies in the cell at Pentonville, and three men die in the Madrid prison. You see a glaring coincidence. So do I. I don't see *more* than a coincidence."

"Go on thinking about it."

"There's nothing to think about. Jones died from one of the many things a condemned man can die of—that condemned men *have* died of, not seldom. What have they got to live for? They tend to give up, emotionally, sometimes physically. If a mid-African forgets to make an obeisance when he walks past a chief's burial-ground he dies within a week, because it's ordained in his tribe's sacred laws. He dies because he's convinced he will; he dies of his own faithful convictions. A man in the death-cell can go out like a light with a common cold, because the bug has attacked something that doesn't want to fight it—"

"Hugo."

"M'm?"

"Come out of Wonderland."

He stopped walking up and down, and stood looking at Miss Gorringe thoughtfully. In a moment he said:

"The report from Madrid isn't reliable on any count. At the last minute there was a change in political opinion, or there was a loophole in the opposition's policy, allowing—"

"There is no opposition in Madrid—"

"Or for some reason known only to Spanish political factions it was desirable to reprieve those three men. But there was the question of face-saving too. So they were given a tot of cyanide before they were led out to the execution yard, and finished up dead but not executed, satisfying the peculiar requirements of political expedience."

Miss Gorringe stared patiently at her perfectly lacquered nails, and in a few seconds said, "So Mr. Bishop has set his heart on a trip to

ROOK'S GAMBIT

Luxembourg, and is dodging a new case."

"There's no new case."

"So be it; there is no new case. Then let there be lunch."

She got up, slipping the newspaper-cutting back into her file.

Bishop took out his *meerschaum* and looked at the bowl, turning it in the light. He heard Miss Gorringe on the phone in the hall, asking for the scampi to be sent up. When she came back he was looking at the newspaper-cutting, his head turned obliquely, his whole attitude disinterested.

"They don't even name the prisoners," he said. "They don't even name the prison."

"It's just a filler," she said, and raised the table-leaf in the dining-alcove, clattering about with cutlery. He put the slip back into its file, slid the file into its drawer, and shut the drawer.

The service-lift was moaning upwards. Chu Yi-Hsin moved her elegant head, listening. These two heathens might, for once, have ordered fish.

Bishop said briefly, "What time is the inquest?"

Miss Gorringe moved the rose-bowl to the table and said blandly, "What inquest?"

"On Jones."

"Oh. I really couldn't say."

He wandered across to the alcove. "Will the Press be there?"

"I imagine so. It's a matter of public concern."

He sat down, and toyed with a bread-roll. She went to the lift and opened the doors, saying over her shoulder:

"Now I remember, the inquest is fixed for three-thirty. But that's a good hour after your plane leaves. Never mind."

Bishop got up and dialled the number of the airline, and canceled his booking, and came back and sat down again. Miss Gorringe said, "As a matter of mere interest, why did you try to dodge me with such pathetic ineptitude?"

"Because this thing looked too interesting to be true."

"And it's your habit to kick a gift-horse in the teeth."

"Something like that."

2nd MOVE

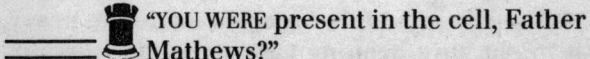"YOU WERE present in the cell, Father Mathews?"

"I was, but I cannot add anything to the testimony of the other two witnesses."

"Even so, we should like to hear what happened, in your own words."

The Padre inclined his head. Bishop was making a pencil-sketch of the Padre's head. One of the very few things Bishop could sketch with any competence was a brick; and this man's head was oblong and brick-red. Perhaps it was working in prisons for so long that had brought this about, over the decades. When he spoke, he showed gaps in his strong elongated teeth. They had become, over the decades, like bars.

"Well, then, I had spent a few minutes outside the cell, talking to the brother of the deceased, Mr. David Jones, and to the other visitor, Dr.

Veiss, whom I understood to be a friend of the condemned man. We went into the cell, and found him talking quietly to one of the warders. He greeted his brother cheerfully, and talked to him for a time, while Dr. Veiss and I waited near the door until there was a chance to approach him."

Bishop looked round the room and tried to place it. There were no bars at the windows, so that it was not any kind of detention-room. The desk where the Coroner sat was a small one with collapsible legs, almost a trestle-table, but heavy; it might have been moved in here for the purpose of this inquest. There were no notices on the walls, nor lettered panels on the doors. The lights were hooded with green metal shades, freezing flat surfaces in an ice-hard light. This might be any room, any nameless room where nameless things were performed; it was a bleak, anonymous room that could be turned into a station-buffet by the tossing in of a few stale buns and a battered tea-urn, or into a sub-post-office by the scattering in of a few crossed nibs and a sad-faced spinster. In this kind of room, the voice of Father Mathews would always sound hollow and unheard, because it was a walled-in wilderness of windows.

"It was when I was in conversation with one of the warders that Jones collapsed. I looked up to see him in the arms of his brother, who had caught him before he could fall to the floor. His brother was saying his name in bewilderment—"

"You didn't actually see him at the instant when he collapsed, Father?"

"Well, no. I heard a scuffle, and by the time I had turned my head to see what was happening, Jones was supported in his brother's arms."

Bishop watched the long brick-red face and the sandy hair. The Coroner said:

"Who was nearest to him?"

"Well, his brother, and the warder who was not talking to me, nearer the door."

"And where was Dr. Veiss?"

Bishop swung his eyes as a little man with gold-rimmed spectacles interrupted, "I was also near the door—"

"If you please, Dr. Veiss. I am questioning Father Mathews."

"I am sorry."

The Coroner nodded, and looked at the Padre. The Padre said:

"Yes, Dr. Veiss was also near the door. He was standing beside me."

Someone coughed, muffling the sound as much as he could in this oasis of silence. The Coroner scratched his ear-lobe. Bishop was watching the little man with the gold-rimmed spectacles.

"So there's nothing you can tell us, Father Mathews, that might suggest the reason for this man's death?"

The Padre said carefully, "We had arranged his death. God was more expedient."

The Coroner did not seem impressed. "There is of course no indication of foul play; that must be ruled out, if only for lack of any evidence. But did it occur to you perhaps that Jones might have taken his life?"

Mathews appeared shocked.

"How, sir?"

"By poison, for instance."

"But the doctor has told us there's no trace of anything noxious in the body—"

"But supposing a poison had been taken—something noxious that left no trace in any of the organs—would it have surprised you?"

"It would. Jones suffered his time bravely. He wasn't a man to take his own way out."

The Coroner seemed relieved. Along the bench where his jury sat, feet shuffled. There was no air in this room.

"Thank you, Father Mathews."

The Padre sat down, still looking vaguely indignant about the suggestion of suicide. The Coroner said:

"I can only now submit to the jury that this is the sum of the evidence to guide you. Natu-

ROOK'S GAMBIT

rally the most important is that of the doctor. You'll remember he told us that there was slight evidence of shock near the heart, and that the nervous system suffered the greater part of this shock. He summed-up by saying that he has seen similar cases, though very rarely, in cardiac disturbances abroad. Well now, will you need to deliberate, before you—"

"No, sir." The foreman of the jury had been waiting for this moment. The ball was in his hands. He could get them all out of here into the fresh air, just with a few words. He felt no responsibility either to Jones or the public. It wasn't important how a man died, when that man was as good as dead already. There were more useful things to do than to stifle in this cheerless room, picking over unimportant bones.

"Then what do you find?"

"We find that Thomas Edward Jones died from heart-failure due to unspecified causes."

The Coroner looked nervous. He said:

"Due to unspecified *natural* causes, or to causes that—"

"Unspecified *natural* causes."

Bishop watched the man in black, brother to dead Jones, a thin fanatical-looking man with his forebears buried in the mines. By the light in his eyes one might imagine he nursed a startling conviction: that Thomas Edward had been caught up into the air by God at his eleventh hour, so that mankind should be saved the stigma of injustice. They had been about to hang the innocent, and the Lord had intervened. It was an answer too simple and too inspiring to ignore. Thomas Edward was never a man born to be hanged, but to be saved by miracles.

"That is all." The Coroner turned to his clerk.

Bishop saw Dr. Veiss get up and move towards the door. The Padre was already there. Two or three of the jury were queueing up to shuffle out. They had decided how Jones had died; it remained for them to decide how to make up for lost time, after this interruption of their daily plans.

When Bishop reached the gates of the prison, he was a few yards behind Dr. Veiss; but there seemed no point, at this stage, in catching him up. He watched him go into the distance.

"Why did he interest you?"

"No clear reason, Gorry. I would have liked to find out what he was doing there, that's all."

"In the cell?"

"Yes."

Miss Gorringe sat efficiently at her desk. Her desk was smaller than the other one that straddled half the window-bay, its length of limed-oak cluttered with Bishop's bric-à-brac. The smaller desk was well-ordered, neatly appointed with the minimum of equipment, and designed, almost, as a setting for Miss Gorringe as she sat there, young in her middle-age, subtly groomed, deft in her movements, happy in her work and in her life. It was round this center of stability that a man like Bishop could best rotate by centrifugal force.

"What's he like, Hugo?"

"Dr. Veiss?"

She nodded. He said, "Pleasant little man with worry on his back—"

"Worry about this Jones affair?"

"Possibly. German extraction, quite an accent, quick in his movements. I should imagine he was some kind of technician."

"Was he a friend of Jones?"

"The Padre said he understood him to be, and no one corrected him. I didn't feel I ought to talk to him at the prison, and there's not much point in finding out his address, because—"

"Twelve, Rider's Lane, West Hampstead."

Bishop bowed his head. She said, "Shouldn't you go and see him?"

"Find out why he was there when Jones died? But Jones died of heart-failure."

"And you've lost interest."

"Not completely, but there's no hint of foul play. At the moment, there's no case." He watched Miss Gorringe patiently. She said:

"Don't cry off, Hugo. Follow through."

"And go to Madrid?"

"It'll make a trip for you, instead of Luxembourg. The weather's good; it's not peak travelling season yet; you like Spain; and—"

"And you think this is a case; you're really convinced."

She nodded neatly. "Yes."

He shrugged. "You've never let me down. I'll buy this one."

Miss Gorringe relaxed. "I'm glad. It could be a corker."

The telephone rang and she picked it up. "Yes?" She passed it to Bishop. "It's Freddie."

Bishop said into the phone, "Good afternoon, Cock. How are you?"

"All right. You?"

"Yes. What d'you want—pick my brains?"

"It'd take a watchmaker. You free tonight, for a meal?"

"Yes—no."

"Well, which?"

"I've just remembered I've got to go to Madrid."

Frisnay said, "Madrid? What for?"

"Smuggle a bunch of onions through the old

Spanish customs. Make it tomorrow night; I should be back by then."

"All right. Where?"

"Here. We can talk better here. I might have something to tell you, about Jones."

"Who?"

"Thomas Edward Jones, the man they couldn't hang."

There was a short silence on the line; then Frisnay said:

"Oh, him. What's he got to do with Madrid?"

"If you could tell me, it'd save my going there."

Frisnay said, "I haven't got a thought on the subject. Jones is a dead duck. I'd say you were running hard up a cul-de-sac."

"Well, I'm fitted with reverse. We'll look forward to seeing you here, about eight tomorrow night. Yes?"

"I'll be charmed. But you won't have anything to tell me about Jones."

"Then I'll regale you with the latest bull-fight scores."

When he had put the phone down he looked at Miss Gorringe and said, "Freddie doesn't often just ring up like that for something to do."

"Especially after you've just been to an inquest at a prison."

"Would he know that I went?"

"If he's following the Jones affair."

"He says there's nothing to follow. He told me I'm up a dead end."

"Maybe he took care to say that. The Yard might be so interested in this glaring coincidence that it doesn't want any public conjecture."

Bishop filled a pipe. He said, "I take it there'll be a plane for Madrid some time today?"

"There is. You're due at the airport at five-thirty—"

"You jump ahead of me, don't you?"

"It keeps me fit—"

"It's nearly five o'clock now. You could have given me a chance to pack."

"You're packed." She got up, shutting a desk drawer and smoothing her skirt. "The bag's by the front-door. Passport with visa in the briefcase, together with traveller's checks and the address of an American newspaper-man in Madrid. His name is Austin. He'll be of some help."

She took a blue cigarette from the box and lit it deftly. "Have a nice trip."

3rd MOVE

THE FOYER of the hotel was cool. Outside, in the street, the stones of pavements and buildings had been warming to a sun that was trying to glare through a heat-mist. Madrid was waiting for its short, intolerable summer; already the people were wilting under the presence of heat that was still not here yet to grill them. For Bishop, the evening was warm in the open, cool in the shade, luxurious after the English spring he had left behind a few hours ago. People glanced up, hearing his light, quick step across the floor-tiles.

He asked at the desk for Mr. Austin, an American. They said Mr. Austin was here, yes. Room Twenty-one. He was shown the lift. The lift went up through the well of the building like a tumbril rising from Hades, its lop-sided cage bumping the runners, sending up a series of small, shrill screams ahead of it, scaring the echoes. Bishop got out, thankful. If he had to climb to the third floor again, he would use the stairs.

Austin, the American, was sitting on a small balcony with faded paint and a sagging striped blind. The balcony looked as safe as the lift had looked. It appeared to shake, as the American's hands went dancing about over the typewriter keys. He said without looking up:

"Have a chair. You English?"

"Yes." Bishop sat down on a wicker chaise-longue that half-pitched him sideways on to the floor. Austin stopped work on his machine and came through the balcony doorway, folding his arms across his sun-vest.

"The other chair's better."

Bishop looked at the other chair. It was an over-stuffed relic of some Northern palace; its arms sprouted some form of shaggy padding through the remains of leather. Austin said, "It's not clean, but it's not dangerous, like that one. Have a drink?"

"I'd like a drink, very much." Bishop looked away from the other, less dangerous chair, and stood up. The wicker-work of the chaise-longue sprang back into former shapelessness.

"I'm drinking Cinzano, Mr.—"

"Bishop. Cinzano's fine."

Austin turned back with the glasses, and looked at Bishop with one slow, three-second take, and said:

"Welcome to Iberia. You look as though you've just got in."

"I do?"

"You haven't started to sweat yet."

They drank a little and he added, "What can I do? And who told you about me? You on the grind?"

"No, I'm a free-lance." He wandered nearer the doorway, where the air seemed cooler. "Last week the London papers carried a story about some political prisoners who were put in front of a firing-squad here—"

"Oh, that one; yes, sure."

"Did you see something of that business, yourself?"

Austin blanked his face a little. "I could have. Not officially, you understand. In fact it's only the London end of my syndicate that knows where the story came from. If these boys knew, they'd sling me across the Pyrenees, frontier formalities waived."

"The Press wasn't invited to the proposed execution?"

"It never is. Not the foreign Press, leastways."

Bishop nodded, and moved back into the room, where the air seemed cooler. He was beginning to sweat now. He was beginning to know what Austin meant, about the climate here. Austin looked at his drink and said, "But I ducked in, under the curtain—you know? Not with the idea of reporting anything. Just wanted to be in on a new scene—new to me, anyway. Just for the experience, you understand? You say you're not a news-man, Mr. Bishop?"

"No, I can't say I am, Mr. Austin."

"You—er—you making some kind of official enquiry, m'm?"

"Not in any way official, no. Just for the experience, you understand?"

Austin grinned slowly. "Oh sure, sure. But, you see, it's difficult. In this country you have to—"

"You've got my word that I still don't know who put that report through to your syndicate, the London end. I don't even know which syndicate it was. The Channel Agency signed it."

"That's right, it did. Then how did you get to me?"

"My secretary mentioned your name."

"That doesn't help any, does it? See, Mr. Bishop, this is a queer country. Nice people, but queer country—speaking politically. A news-man has to keep his nose clean if he's going to stay here any length of time longer than ten seconds; and I aim to; I'm sunk on the place. So..."

Bishop opened his jacket. "Is it any cooler on the balcony?"

"Only when you jump off it, and get the rush of air."

Bishop took his jacket off and passed a cigarette, and said, "I can't expect you to tell me anything until I put myself more clearly in the picture for you. I write books. You could call them case-books. They come under the group-title of *Personality under Stress*. I look for my material in odd places, and—"

"H. B. Ripton—check?"

"That's my pseudonym, yes."

"Now that's something like an introduction. I know your books. Have another drink, as a privilege to me."

"No, this is fine. You go ahead."

Austin refilled his glass. He said, "Now you can ask."

"I'd just like to know what you saw in that execution yard. If you feel like telling me— well, you know my name, and you can ask me any time to return the service."

"Sure. It's nice to have friends who pick up their material in odd places. I'm going to tell you everything—but that's not much."

He sprawled suddenly across the wicker chair, which somehow seemed to support him. He said in a moment:

"There were the three guys against the wall. There was the armed squad and its officer. There were a few other guys just standing around— a routine execution committee, I guess, with a good helping of priests. There were a couple of boys who might have been press-men. And there was me. They didn't see much of me."

"You were somewhere in the background."

"I was somewhere in the background.... I'd seen these three guys brought into the yard. Two priests stayed with them for quite a time, giving them absolution or just making them feel it was all going to turn out okay in the end. Then they were blindfolded and propped against the wall."

His pleasant Brooklyn voice, its accent pithy as a bouncing ball, broke off for a moment and he looked at Bishop. Then he said off-handedly, "You ever seen a firing-squad, Mr. Bishop?"

"Yes."

"Then you know the scene. I needn't describe it. Was it in Spain?"

"No. Italy."

"How did you sneak in?"

"I didn't. They led me in, with six other men. We were at the receiving end of the performance. It was in the war."

"You don't say. How did you skip before they—"

"We didn't all skip, Mr. Austin. There was—" He held out his empty glass. "I'll join you now, I think. You were saying?"

Austin filled his glass and came back with it and said:

"Yes, sure. Well, I saw the firing-squad form up. They waited for the command. We all waited for that, I guess. I stood there trying to work out the morality of the thing, but of course I couldn't; it has no morality you could ever give a decent name to. Suicide, by those three guys, would have been the unforgivable sin, greater than any crime on earth, according to their religious beliefs. But this wasn't even a crime at all. It was legal, orderly murder."

He watched Bishop tilt his glass, became lost in a twist of thought, groped his way back and said, "Then it happened. I had to stop philosophizing pretty fast because the scene had changed. Most of it remained just about the same. It was frozen—*we* were frozen by our surprise. A second back three blindfolded men had been standing against the wall. Now they were spreadeagled on the ground, dead." He shrugged. "And I'd been watching, you understand? I hadn't been looking around, anywhere else. I watched them fall. They fell dead. They fell like stones."

Bishop waited. Austin became lost again. Cries of children came floating through the window, touching their ears. Bishop said:

"Without a sound."

The American looked up. "Without a sound. As if they'd fainted. After that strange moment of frozen amazement people ran towards them. The priests were there; the doctors were there; the press-boys were there, picking up the bodies, propping them against the wall, as if they'd come back to life in a minute. All I heard was the same bewildered phrase, repeated and repeated, *'Son muertos—son muertos!'* And, brother, it was no lie. They were as dead as stones."

Bishop was watching his face. There was still the faint reflection of surprise in it, as he remembered how it had been, there in the yard by the prison.

"What's your answer?"

He said to Bishop, "There are several. Any could fit. They were poisoned without their knowing it—but why should anyone poison them when there was a firing-squad rigged up? They took poison themselves, delayed-action stuff—but why? A Spaniard doesn't take his life just because someone else is going to do it, especially if he's a good Catholic. What's the point? They know all about death, here. They live with it; they got it into perspective a long time ago. They're not scared of death, only of dying; and a bullet's quicker than poison, and often less painful. Those guys didn't take anything, you've got my word. What else? Heart-failure. It's the only thing you can say, isn't it?"

"That would do, for one of them. Not for three. You know why I've come over here?"

"We-ell, seeing you're interested in this business, I'd say it was on account of that guy Jones, in Pentonville."

"Correct. I hoped it might be news to you, that you could use."

Austin moved his head. "I had a flash come through. If I weren't on a general assignment I'd take a crack at this story, because it tingles. But I can't give it the time."

Bishop said, "You were working when I came. I'll leave you in peace."

"That's okay. I'm working most of the time. It was a nice break. You going on checking, back in England?"

"Yes. I suddenly don't believe in heart-failure."

"If you can give this thing a better name, let me know. I'd really be interested."

"I won't fail to do that." He put his jacket on.

"You going to be long in Madrid?"

"I have to be back in London by tomorrow evening."

"Then you're flying. You can do something for me?"

"Anything."

Austin said, "There's a girl here, from London, on vacation. She's English, works for some paper, on the editorial side. I met up with her at the international press-club here."

"She's in trouble?"

"How did you know? She's lost her passport, or the visa's over-run, something like that—we couldn't talk very well because I was in a hurry and the place was crowded—and anyway there's not much I can do because I'm American and she's not. You're English. Do I give you the address?"

"Please."

"It's a small hotel—small as this one but not so broken-down. In the Plaza Menor, Calle del Sol."

"Her name is?"

"Vic Levinson."

Bishop moved towards the door. "I'll see her, and do what I can. Mr. Austin, you've been a great help."

"No, but I tried. I imagine you'll find yourself, by chance, near the prison where it happened?"

"By sheer chance."

"They won't let you inside, brother."

"I think I'd rather they didn't. Where is it?"

"In Calle San José. It's a small gaol for—er—particular cases."

"I'll find it."

He thanked Austin and left. Going down the stairs, he heard the typewriter start up again. The sound of it followed him down, diminishing slowly like a distant rattle of bullets, trapped between walls.

MOVE

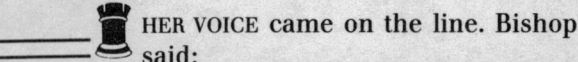 HER VOICE came on the line. Bishop said:

"Miss Levinson?"

"Speaking." She sounded pleased.

"I'm afraid this isn't the call you've been waiting for. Shall I ring off, and clear the line?"

"I don't understand."

"You sounded so glad—and I'm a stranger."

"Oh. I was glad to hear an English voice on my telephone. My Spanish doesn't go down very well. They think it's Chinese. I don't blame them—it sounds like Chinese to me too."

"I see." He pictured her as small, dark, with clear eyes and quick nerves. But voices were deceptive. He said, "My name is Bishop. Mr. Austin told me you were in a slight fix about your papers—"

"Slight? Have you ever tried getting help from the Guardia Civil?"

"They're very helpful; but they don't understand Chinese. I suggest we meet, and I'll see if there's anything I can do."

"You're an angel from Heaven."

"No, just a Bishop from London. Shall I come round to your hotel?"

She hesitated and then said, "No. I'll come to you. I need fresh air. I've been two hours on this telephone, trying to get the British Consulate. So far I've got three museums, a night-club, and the bull-ring. Where are you?"

"Hotel Internacional, near the Puerto de la Luna. Will you be able to find it?"

"I'll try. Near the Puerto de la what?"

"De la Luna. The Gate of the Moon."

"It sounds wonderful in any language. I'll get there as soon as I can. Will you wait for me?"

Bishop said, "Yes. Here, or at the bull-ring, or one of the museums?"

Her laugh was delightful, even over the wires.

She was half an hour. Bishop was waiting for her on the steps of his hotel, watching the night come down across the mountain tops and the frieze of roofs. His feet were aching. As she came across the road and looked at the hotel entrance he said:

"You did well. It's a good five minutes, from your place."

"You're Mr. Bishop?"

"Yes."

She looked surprised. "You're not like you sounded. You didn't sound so young, or so—" She moved her hands quickly. "Sorry I took so long. I got on the wrong bus."

"That was better than the wrong ship."

Her laugh was delightful to look at, too. "I'm hopeless, aren't I?"

"Yes. I find it rather appealing. I suggest we stroll across the square, while we talk. There's a pleasant little restaurant there, with a cabaret. Or have you had something?"

"No, I—but aren't we going to the Consulate?"

"At eleven o'clock at night?"

"Don't they keep open for emergencies?" She was worried. He thought that was appealing, too. And she was dark, and less than five and a half feet tall. The picture hadn't been very much out of focus.

He said, as they began walking slowly across the square:

"This may be an emergency for you. It isn't for the British Consulate."

"But it'll be too late tomorrow."

"In this country, more than in any other, tomorrow never comes. Likewise, it is never too late."

Her dark head swung to look at him. "But if I don't get back by Monday morning, my job goes right out of the editor's window."

He said, "I have to be back by eight o'clock tomorrow evening, Sunday. If I promise to take you with me, will you relax?"

"How do I know I can rely on you?"

"It's a challenge to your judgment. Take your time."

She looked up at him again, and then said, "I'll risk it, and relax. You have a persuasive charm. Are you a con-man?"

"How did you know?"

He steered her across the street as she was about to get into a fast-moving taxi, and found a table in the restaurant.

She said, "It's nice." She didn't seem so worried now. She watched the little fountain that was splashing in the middle of the room. Its jet was veering sideways a little, and a waiter was watching it too, trying to make up his mind whether to turn off the water, straighten the pipe, or hope it would right itself. He had been doing this for three years, between waiting at the tables.

Bishop and the girl stayed until two o'clock. The food had been good; the cabaret had been spasmodic. A man was singing now, moving round the great stone bowl of the fountain as he sang.

She said, when he had gone, "What was he singing?"

"A love-song. He said that the words he sang would fly to the moon, and echo back to his beloved, so that she would hear them, wherever she was."

Quietly she murmured, "How wonderful." She looked up. "I'll be sorry to leave here. Really sorry."

"Spain?"

"Yes."

"When did you come?"

"Only three days ago. It was Spain or the Lake District. I have an aunt in the Lake District."

"So you came to Spain."

"Yes." When she smiled, her eyes lit. He watched them. She asked: "What about you? Is this Mr. Austin a friend of yours?"

"No. I came to see him about a story."

She was alerted. "Yes?"

"I was forgetting—you're a reporter, too."

"In a minor key. Garden fêtes and council meetings, the whole mediocre round that no one else wants to do."

"Why do you do it?"

"Someone must. It doesn't worry me, only bores me. What story did you come to see Mr. Austin about? Can I ask that?"

He said, "Yes, I think so. There were three prisoners, who fell dead in—"

"That story. Yes, I heard about it."

"Well, there's been another one, in London. A man fell dead at eight o'clock this morning. He was to have been hanged at nine."

Her eyes widened. She said nothing. He murmured:

"It's what they call a coincidence."

Her voice had gone a little bleak with shock. "But they were all—"

"They were all condemned men who died, yes. That's what interests me."

"Are you on a paper?"

"No. I'm just interested. I'd like to find out why these men died; and find out how."

"This is—really a big story, isn't it?"

He nodded. She said:

"How can you find out anything over here? They won't give you facilities."

"Over here you find things out the same way as you find things out anywhere. By looking round. That's what I've been doing this evening, before I rang you."

She was still alerted. The shock had passed, the shock of hearing about Jones in a setting like this. "Will you tell me?"

"I don't see why not." He lit a cigar. "The prison is in Calle San José. The walls are bounded on two sides by narrow streets. Many of the houses are fifth-rate boarding-places, because there's a pleasant little park nearby, and the view is nice. I spent an hour in the quarter, looking for rooms—the highest rooms, the attics, under the roof. I went on to the roof itself, having engineered a situation that left me to my own devices for a moment. The view from the roof is also nice, in the Calle San José, right at the end of the street. You can see, obliquely, right into the prison yard, if you've a head for heights."

Two women, in Andalucian costume, were dancing now, moving round the fountain. The clack of their castanets broke brittle echoes against the walls. The girl watched Bishop, vaguely aware of the rhythm of the dance. She said in a moment:

"I'm perhaps not very bright. Do I miss a point?"

Bishop was looking at the dancers. They danced flamenco. He said, turning his head back, "There isn't any real point yet. Call it a piece of a pattern, and keep it by you." His tone didn't change as he said, "It's nice to have someone like you to talk to. It helps me to work things out. And I can trust your discretion."

Their eyes held for a second. She said with a slow nod:

"Yes, you can trust me."

The dancers stamped their feet, whirling the castanets above their heads, swinging them down. The sound rippled, shivering in the crowded room.

"At these places," Bishop said, "I also enquired for a friend of mine. That was how I described him. It wasn't easy, because I didn't know which of two men I was looking for, and I didn't think there was a chance in blazes of finding him anyway. You see, there were five men with Jones when he fell dead this morning: two warders, the padre, his own brother, and a man named Veiss. I was looking for Jones—the brother—or Veiss. A friend of mine ... from England ... staying in Madrid last week ... could the Señora recall such a man? No, but there was a German. She didn't know, this particular Señora at this particular *pension*, which was the tenth I'd called at—she didn't know where the German had come from. Germany would be a natural guess. I described him."

The English girl looked away once, as the dancers stopped and the cries of *Ole!* went up; then she looked back to Bishop. He was glad she didn't interrupt. He wanted to work things out while he talked. While he talked his mind was running over the whole pattern, as the left hand runs over the keyboard while the right hand picks the tune.

"My description was accurate. Yes, the German was short, and wore gold-rimmed spectacles, and had not much hair. And yes, the name in the register was Dr. Veiss. But alas, my friend had gone away."

She said, "Was he staying here last week, near the prison, when those three men died?"

"Yes. And this morning he was at Pentonville, when Jones fell down dead."

On her breath she said, "This is fantastic."

"If it weren't, it wouldn't interest me."

"You were very quick in coming here to Madrid. What will you do now?"

"Be very quick in going back to London. And call on Veiss."

An inch of ash fell from his Habana. She said, "I should like to walk."

He paid the bill and they left the restaurant. The square was quieter now, and their footsteps were clear along the paving-stones; but voices came sometimes calling, sometimes singing, from behind windows, beyond rooftops, clearly in the airless night.

A lean bitch ran past them, its teeth bared and ribs showing under the thin fur; it ran down towards the slum quarter to root out garbage, desperate not to starve to death, as it had been since it was born, as it would do till it died. A voice came, more loudly than the others—a woman singing half in her sleep, somewhere high among the soft white walls. She sang of love, because she had never been in love, and neither her faith nor her ten children would let her know it now.

"Hugo . . . "

"Yes?"

"Who are you?"

"It depends where I am and whom I'm with."

The square was shadowed, under clear stars. He touched her hand, turning her towards the wide street that led to her hotel. She said in a moment:

"I don't know if it's the food I've had, or the wine we drank, but I feel out of my depth. You've talked for a long time about death, and already it doesn't seem horrible. I'm not even sure I can go home with you tomorrow; and if I can't, I'll lose my job; and I can't care, tonight. I don't even care, much, who you are. But I like you."

"I'm glad."

"It's not a very generous word, 'like'."

"It means what it says."

"Where are we going?"

He said, "To your hotel."

"This is the way?"

"Yes."

"It'll have changed, my little hotel."

"Are they redecorating it?"

Her smile sounded in her voice. "I shan't feel the same about it, now, as I did when I left it."

"Then it's you who's been redecorated."
"Yes."
"And you're half-asleep."
"Yes."
"Shall I carry you the rest of the way?"
"No; they'd think I was drunk."

They came to the steps, after minutes without speaking.

"Is this my hotel?"
"Yes," he said.

She stood in front of him, looking up at his face.

"Are you going back now, to yours?"

He nodded. She said, "I'm sorry."

"Are you?"

"I'm feeling so wonderfully redecorated, and when you leave me the feeling will stop."

"Which floor are you on?"

"The first."

He said, "Then we needn't use the lift. I get worried in these lifts over here. I don't think they work very well."

They climbed the steps slowly.

"I'm not behaving very well, Hugo, am I?"

"I think you're behaving beautifully."

5th
MOVE

♜ "PASSENGERS FOR Lisbon, Dakar, Natal, and Rio de Janeiro please be prepared—"

The voice was cut off as the door of the kiosk closed. The coins went in; he pressed the button; the coins rang down with a discordant tintinnabulation. Miss Gorringe came on:

"Hello?"

"Gorry—Hugo. Just landed."

"Welcome home."

"Thank you. Has Freddie rung up?"

"No. Should he have?"

"I hoped he might have had to work late, and so cancel our dinner tonight. I'm a fraction pressed. What time did we say?"

Miss Gorringe said, "Eight. It's now six forty-five. Do you want me to phone him and—"

"No. I'll be there. I'm calling, first, on Dr.

Veiss. Twelve, Rider's Lane, West Hampstead. Check?"

"Check. Why call on Veiss?"

"He was staying at a house overlooking the prison in Madrid when those three men died—"

"Good grief!"

"I'll tell you the rest this evening. We'll have to hurry now."

She asked. "Who is 'we'?"

"Oh—I brought a girl back with me. Rather a comely little orphan of the storm."

With resignation Miss Gorringe said, "Bishop rides again. Do I prepare the guest-room?"

"Unfortunately, she has a home. I'm about to escort her there."

"And that's why you're a fraction pressed. I won't keep you."

"Look forward to seeing you for dinner, at eight."

He rang off.

Vic Levinson lived in a room in Kensington Park Way. He stood with her on the porch of the house while the taxi's engine idled in the background.

"I still don't believe I'm home, or that I've still got a job to go to in the morning. You've been very kind, Hugo."

"It gave me great pleasure. If you ever find yourself in Madrid again, please lose your passport and send me a wire."

"In Chinese?"

"Just say, 'Require redecorating'. "

She looked at him for a moment and then said, "You must go now. Tell me, tomorrow or some time, what happened when you saw Dr. Veiss. On the phone would do."

He turned down the steps. She said as if without wanting to, "I feel more lost, just now, than I ever did in Madrid."

He stood on the pavement. Against the dark door she looked slighter than ever, and—yes, a little bit lost.

"You came in almost at the beginning of this story, Vic. If you want to follow it through, would your paper use it?"

"Exclusive?"

"First on the street."

"You mean that?"

"As far as it's in my hands. I'll keep you informed."

They didn't call good-bye. She was no longer standing there when the taxi drove away. The dark door was just closing.

Twelve, Rider's Lane was a small 1930's villa, detached, well-painted, with a neat front path. Lamplight cast the shadow of a rowan-tree across the porch. The door was opened within a few seconds of Bishop's ring; the boy who answered it must have been passing through the hall, or perhaps waiting for someone to call, someone who was expected, not Bishop. The boy was about eighteen, tall, blond-headed, nervous-eyed as he stared at Bishop, trying to place him.

Bishop said, "Good evening."

"Good evening." Nerves in the voice, too.

"I wonder if Dr. Veiss might give me a moment? My name is Bishop."

After a brief hesitation, "Come in."

In the dim-lighted hall the boy said with a soft jerk, "Is it about Marilyn?"

Bishop said, "Marilyn?"

A woman's voice came. "Derek, who is that?"

The boy was still watching Bishop, waiting for an answer. Bishop turned and looked at the woman who was coming down the stairs. She didn't look like this boy's mother. The boy said briefly, "Someone to see Father."

"Please go to your room."

He went up the stairs, his shoulders resigned.

The woman said with less asperity, "I am Mrs. Veiss. Who are you, please?" Her accent was as marked as her husband's.

"My name is Bishop. I wondered if Dr. Veiss might see me for a moment."

She seemed put-out. "Yes. What about, please? He is very busy."

"I see." It would be necessary to shoot in the dark. "I'm just back from Madrid, Mrs. Veiss."

"Madrid? I do not understand."

"Dr. Veiss was there last week."

He thought her surprise was genuine. "In Madrid? I do not think so. You had better see him. It is this way."

As she opened the door of the room, Veiss began speaking to her from inside. This was obviously not a house where stray visitors were at liberty.

"Olga, you must tell that boy that if he wishes to—"

"Hermann, this is Mr. Bishop. To see you."

She stood to one side. Veiss said with irritation, "But I am busy, Olga. You must—" He broke off, looking up from a narrow, littered desk on which a bronze lamp burned. "For a moment, then, please."

"I'm sorry to call at an awkward time, Dr. Veiss."

The woman left them, closing the door. Veiss stood up, taking his spectacles off, frowning against the light as it struck upwards through the top of the shade. The shadow of his head sprang against the wall, a vast, softly delineated egg.

"Awkward," he said, "yes. Our boy is difficult. He is a worry to us."

Bishop could only imagine that Veiss thought he had overheard raised voices, minutes ago in this house, and that it must be explained, even apologized for.

"It's a worrying age," Bishop said. "They spread their wings and go crashing head-first out of the nest, don't they?"

That must be somewhere on the right track. There was woman-trouble named Marilyn. The boy was too handsome and virile-looking to be a model son at his age. He felt rather sorry for Derek.

"Their wings, yes." Veiss seemed only vaguely in touch with the present. "Out of the nest. That is an English proverb, Mr. Bishop?"

"Not exactly."

"Now you wish to talk to me?"

"For a moment, if I may. I notice you recognize me, Dr. Veiss."

"Yes. Yes—you were at the inquest yesterday. But sit down, please." He put his glasses back; their gold rims glinted in the light. "I—I have not told my family that I was present when— the man Jones—it is a morbid thing, and—"

"I understand, yes."

"Thank you, sir."

Bishop looked at the room from the chair. A

technician's room, with many reference books about, frequently used; here and there a piece of electrical equipment; a massive television set, with the back open, wired to some recording device; here and there an attempt by Mrs. Veiss to establish that this was in fact the living-room: heavy brocaded curtains, ornaments of such a size and number to dwarf, or at least camouflage, the ugly pieces of equipment that were one of the banes of her life. The other appeared to be Derek.

Bishop said, "I have also been to Madrid."

Veiss paused in the chasing of some thought through his mind.

"Madrid?" He wandered unhappily round the room and then said, "I will sit down. I am very busy."

Bishop waited. He wished he had not come, or had at least come at a better time, when Veiss was not working, or worrying about the boy. He had come with a third problem.

"I am a radio—" he worked the word out carefully—"I am a radiophysicist." He became nervously amused: "It took me a long time to learn that word, you see—"

"Your English is almost perfect, Doctor—"

"Oh no, please. Yet I am British. All my family. After the war—but that is of no interest." The silence drew out. For the first time he seemed to settle his thoughts on one definite track. "You say you have been to Madrid, Mr. Bishop."

"Yes."

"It was for a vacation?" The polite smile was frozen.

"No. I went to the street by the prison, in Calle San José."

Veiss looked at his hands. Visibly, he was bringing his mind to bear on the situation, pushing other problems aside while he concentrated. His attitude, his whole body seemed to become steady. He was a technician streamlining his complete attention to focus on the one vital fact.

"I have not been there, Mr. Bishop. I have never been to Madrid. So I cannot be of help to you."

Bishop took his *meerschaum* from a pocket. He began filling the bowl. "Would Mrs. Veiss mind if I lit a pipe in her house?"

The question, so divorced from the subject, almost startled the little man; but he recovered.

"No. Please light your pipe. But I cannot help you with this—with your problem."

Slowly Bishop said, as he filled the pipe, "I was there last night, in the Calle San José. I talked to Señora Lopez, at Number Nineteen—that is right at the end of the street: the little *pension* with the blue balconies. The name of Dr. Veiss was in her register. The good Señora described you, precisely. She said you stayed there last week." It was cruel to persist, in this measured tone, in the face of the blank unhappy stare. There was no pitting of wits here. He had invaded a household already disturbed, and was showing no mercy. He felt as unhappy as Veiss. But Veiss had been with Jones, had been in the street by the little prison in Madrid. "She said you were staying there, in her *pension*, at the time when they tried to execute three men in the prison yard across the street, and failed."

He zipped his tobacco pouch and put it away, feeling for a match. "But perhaps I'm making a stupid mistake, Doctor. Perhaps you have a double, of the same name."

Veiss got up, and stood for a moment in the middle of the room. For this moment, Bishop pictured him suddenly as a man standing among his possessions—possessions which had just been packed aside for transportation to somewhere not yet known. As if the whole house was suddenly for sale; as if this man's whole life were up for auction, because he could no longer afford to run it.

Bishop struck a match.

Veiss said without looking at him, "I respect your intelligence too much to pretend you are mistaken. I will only tell you this. Go away, and do not come again. Do not think of this again. Otherwise you will be in great danger. You might lose your life."

Bishop said evenly, "But I'm not due for hanging, or a firing-squad."

Veiss said nothing.

"It's they who seem in most danger, isn't it? Condemned men."

Veiss said, "You must go, please."

Bishop said, getting up from the chair, "I'd be impolite to stay, having been asked to leave, Dr. Veiss. I'll thank you for your warning, and assure you I shall forget it the moment I leave here."

Veiss nodded. He looked happier. He said, "You are wise. I am glad."

Bishop said gently, "I mean that I shall forget your warning."

He moved for the door. He heard, behind him, Veiss moving too. He looked round instinctively; but the little man was still in the middle of the room.

Quietly Bishop murmured, "It's this way out, I think—?"

"I am sorry. I will show you."

Veiss closed the front-door before his visitor had reached the gate. The night was quiet. Lamps cast pools of light along the street. Three cars stood there, parked, unattended. A cat went quickly across a fence, dropping from sight. Far away there was the drone of traffic, and Bishop looked at his watch, remembering. He had fifteen minutes. In a taxi it would take all of that; but he did not move. He stood there, just outside the gate, for longer than a minute, his head fixed, his eyes watching. Then he moved along the pavement, walking steadily.

There was a telephone box on the next corner. He went in. When he had got the number he said:

"Gorry—Hugo. I've just left Dr. Veiss. Tell Freddie I might be a few minutes late for our dinner-party, as I'm being followed. I want to find out why."

"Followed? By Dr. Veiss?"

"No. Nor by his wife, nor their son. This one hasn't a name."

He rang off, came out of the telephone box, and walked south, towards Maida Vale.

6th MOVE

"WHEN DID he ring?"
"Half an hour ago."
Frisnay grunted. Miss Gorringe said:
"If you're hungry, we'll start."
"Oh, no, he won't be long."
"Have another appetizer."
"Thanks."

He stood in front of the Adam hearth; his stance and his build suited the smooth stone; it made a good background. Frisnay was as solid as that stone, as well-proportioned; but he was not so old as it, and he was less smooth. He had once answered a titled matron whom he had unwittingly affronted in the course of an enquiry: "Madam, I am a policeman in the service of Her Majesty, and not a hired smarmer-down of the over-sensitive. You should have called in the Diplomatic Corps, not me." This was the closest approach he had ever made to repartee. In his work he was far less clumsy. He said now, "I suppose Hugo's off on some damn'-silly lark, is he?"

She passed him his glass, refilled.

"That could be a phrase for it, but I think this is something real. He'll tell you the details when he comes."

"I was afraid of that."

Miss Gorringe sat down on the davenport; as a background, it suited her as well as the hearth suited Frisnay. Miss Gorringe had been born to sit on davenports, and the terrace at the Windsor Club, and in the front of Bishop's grey Rolls-Royce. She drifted towards these places with instinctive choice, and graced them with distinction. She sipped her drink.

"You don't look any older, Freddie."

"Than when?"

"Oh, years ago. Your work's probably good for you."

"It'll kill me, one day."

He didn't mean that. It would kill him, if he stopped.

She heard a taxi in the mews below. "Here's Hugo. I hope he's alone. The table's laid for three."

"He liable to bring someone?"

"Slightly. He brought back a memento of Madrid."

Frisnay grunted. "A woman?"

"Dear old Freddie—would he bring back a plastic duck?"

Bishop came into the room.

" 'Lo, Gorry; 'lo, Freddie. Sorry I'm late."

They studied him. He had not been in any kind of *fracas*. That was something. And he was alone. That was something else.

"We're having a drink, before we eat."

"Splendid! Where's mine?"

She got up, and poured him a sherry. Frisnay rocked on his heels in front of the hearth and looked at Bishop and said, "Gorry told me you were being shadowed. Where's the shadow?"

"He gave me the slip." He took his drink. Frisnay said:

"You mean you gave him the slip."

"No, we reversed order, after a time. I wanted to find out who he was, but he melted."

"Any ideas?"

"He might have been anyone."

"This thing you're working on—what's it like?"

"Shapeless, at this stage."

Frisnay brought his drink to the table in the alcove, and they sat down. He said, "I've heard the bit about the three Spaniards, from Gorry. I know, officially, about the death of Jones."

"And you'd call the whole thing a coincidence."

Frisnay nodded. Bishop said, "Gorry doesn't. Nor do I now."

"Now?"

"There's a common factor. His name's Veiss. He's an ex-German British national, wife and son in Hampstead. Last week he was staying at a place directly overlooking the prison in Madrid. Yesterday he was visiting Jones, in Pentonville, when he fell dead."

Frisnay's wooden face registered nothing. Miss Gorringe said, "Look at Freddie. He's interested."

"How can you tell?"

"He's looking bored."

Frisnay grunted. "You've seen this man Veiss, have you?"

"Twice. At the inquest, and at his house tonight."

"Well?"

"He warned me off."

"How seriously?"

"Oh, he was quite pleasant about it. He said if I called there again I might be advised to stop off at the undertaker's and get fitted for a coffin, on the way. Or words roughly to that effect."

Frisnay speared a black olive and said in a moment:

"What's the family like?"

"Odd. The wife seems a nice little woman, but

very upset about the boy. The boy seems a good enough chap, but is very upset about Marilyn."

"Who's Marilyn?"

"I don't know. Her name was mentioned."

"Was it the boy who followed you?"

"No. Jolly sort of cove. Very fat. You got any fat friends, Freddie?"

Frisnay nibbled a grape. Miss Gorringe passed him the salad-bowl. Bishop said, "Listen. Gorry and I want to go to work on this case. If it turns out to be the sort of case it looks like turning out to be, the Yard is going to be in it, up to the ear-lobes."

Frisnay's face went as wooden as it could ever go, which was practically two-dimensional. He said, "So you want me to give you a hand, before I'm in it officially."

"We-ell, it's a rather nice salad. And after that, it's duck. I must say Gorry has taken a lot of trouble to study your palate, and the wine I've chosen was bottled at the château. Besides which—"

"What d'you want?" asked Frisnay.

"Information on Dr. Hermann Veiss."

"When?"

"There's a telephone over there. You could play with it, while you're sipping your brandy, in about half an hour from now."

"I'm a sucker," said Frisnay.

"Yes."

ROOK'S GAMBIT

Bishop was setting out the chessboard. Miss Gorringe was clearing the table. Frisnay listened for another minute at the telephone and then put it down. He said:

"Born German, now British by naturalization. Derek Veiss is an adopted son. He was actually the son of a Gestapo man who saved the lives of Dr. and Mrs. Veiss, losing his own after an indiscretion a few weeks before the war. I imagine this is their way of repaying the debt. Veiss is now working for a television-research company. Good at his job. Derek is a member of a group calling itself World Trust, probably Red."

Bishop looked at the chessboard. He said:

"The parents must have had a pretty clean sheet, to be granted naturalization."

"They must." Frisnay sipped his brandy. "I seem to remember the boy was in some kind of trouble last year. He was monkeying with student-politics and got into a brawl. One of our chaps was knifed, not badly; but it made the whole thing more serious, and the kid who used the knife was sent in."

"No wonder the Veisses are worried about little Derek." Bishop turned the chessboard on the table and said, "Who's taking me on?"

"You and Gorry play. I'll take the winner."

"All right." The telephone rang. Bishop said, "Damn."

Miss Gorringe answered it, and passed it to Bishop. She said with her hand over the mouthpiece, "It's the rather comely little orphan of the storm."

"Bless her heart." Into the phone he said, "Hello, Vic?"

Vic said quickly, "I can't talk for long, Hugo. I've been through my files at the office, digging things up. The name of Veiss rang a bell with me, but it's the son, not the Doctor. Shall I go on?"

"Yes."

"I'll have to be quick. Son's name is Derek. He's a member of a political group called World Trust. There's a meeting tonight. I made a phone-call or two, and as far as anyone knows he'll be at the meeting."

"What time?"

"Quarter past eight to quarter past ten. It's at the Shaftesbury Hall, Pimlico. I'm going to be there. Does any of this interest you?"

Bishop looked at the chessboard and said, "Yes, the bit about your going to be there. I'll drift along about ten o'clock. Then we can compare notes."

"Do try, Hugo. We might be on to something."

"I'll be there."

When he put the receiver back he said, "Freddie—"

"Would I mind," Frisnay grunted, "if you popped off at a quarter to ten? Not in the least. I'd much prefer a game of chess with Gorry to watching you pace up and down."

Bishop said, "Have a cigar."

"I'm incorruptible." Frisnay took a half-Corona and looked at it critically. He said, "That stuff wasn't much use to you, was it? The dope on Veiss I gave you?"

"At the moment, not much. Later, it will be."

Frisnay lit the cigar and said casually, "Let me know if you find out anything tonight."

"Would it interest you?"

"That depends. It might never interest me officially, because I won't necessarily be given the job of following up; but I'm always attracted to the peculiarities of life, which is why I've always looked upon you as my best friend. You're a collector of them."

"I like a man," Bishop said, "who always knows which way his nest is buttered."

"You mean bread is feathered, surely."

A man was speaking. He was a thin, nervous man with bright eyes. He looked doped by his own eloquence. He moved his hands frequently, clenching them, shaking them, clasping them together and tugging them apart as he jerked his feet backwards and forwards on the tiny stage. Except for the raw, shrill voice, he might have been a giant marionette. He was speaking about the Rights of Humanity. It was a large subject.

Fewer than a hundred people were here, but all, or nearly all, listened intently. The atmosphere was cloyed with sympathy. The thin, shrill man was voicing their mass opinion; he was telling them nothing new, nor was he convincing them with his argument: it was also theirs. This was their communal voice, and they were enchanted by it.

The fat man leaned against the wall, half-way down the bleak, low-ceilinged, camphor-smelling hall. He watched the speaker, except when anyone in the audience moved; then he turned his head to watch whoever had moved.

The slim, dark girl was on the far side from the fat man. He knew she was there, but he never looked across at her. She had not seen him.

Bishop murmured, "Don't move, sweetheart. We're being watched."

She caught her breath as he spoke, because he had reached her side silently and she had not seen him come in. Slowly, her pulse decelerated. She said softly:

"How did you get in?"

"Disguised as a mouse. Is the boy here?"

"Derek? Yes. Near the front. Who's watching us?"

"The fat man."

She moved her head, her eyes. After minutes she murmured:

"Where?"

"Opposite, against the wall."

"Who is he?"

"I don't know. He followed me away from Veiss's house tonight. I tried to trip him, but he was too good. Stay just here, won't you?"

"Where are you going?"

"To talk to him."

"Be careful."

He moved away from her. Across the heads of the audience, she could see the fat man turn very slightly, with a natural movement that was perfectly done.

The speaker stopped. Applause beat in waves across the low ceiling, engulfing him; he wallowed in it. A few people hurried forward to the stage, their hands held out. The folding-chairs were banging as the audience stood up. The applause lingered. Through its ebbing sound, Bishop spoke quietly:

"Good evening."

The fat man did not turn his head. He said:

"Good evening."

They stood together, neither looking at the other.

"It's nice weather," Bishop said, "for this time of the year."

"I beg your pardon?"

"I said who the blazes are you?"

The fat man said, "Me? Oh, I vary."

"Human chameleon."

"That's right. You enjoy the meeting, Mr. Bishop?"

"I've only just got here."

"Ah. We started off a bit damp, but finished up lively."

"Yes? So you've been here all the time. Are you on business or pleasure?"

The fat man looked at his shoes.

"Business is pleasure, with me."

People were moving for the doors. Someone banged the push-bar and the doors clattered open. Bishop asked:

"Who are you watching? Derek Veiss?"

"Oh, I watch all of them. Everybody's interesting, don't you think, Mr. Bishop?" He turned his strong, squat body, his hands folded behind him. "Well," he said, "that appears to be all, doesn't it?" He joined the crowd of people who had begun shuffling towards the back of the hall. "G'night, Mr. Bishop. See you again p'r'aps, eh?"

"That wouldn't surprise me. Good night."

He watched the fat man go. He seemed to be in no hurry. He might have been here just to listen to the speeches. Bishop did not believe this. He looked round quickly. Derek Veiss was jumping down from the stage. He would be one of the last to leave. Vic was in the place where Bishop had left her. He made his way slowly across the tide of people.

"Hugo, who was he?"

"He didn't say."

"What did you talk about?"

"The weather." He touched her hand. "Vic, do something for me."

"Yes?"

"I want to know where the Veiss boy goes. If the fat man follows him, we'll just keep in the background. If he doesn't, I want to know where he goes, too. In that case I'll take him on; you take the boy. Derek knows me; he doesn't know you. When you've seen where he's gone, phone my number and give the message. All right?"

"Suppose I lose him?"

"Don't."

Miss Gorringe moved her Queen.

"Check."

Frisnay said, "You're in form tonight."

"I'm feeling relaxed. My Bishop's where I want him."

"You mean your Queen."

"I mean dear old Hugo. He's got some work to do. When there's no case on it's like having an unexploded bomb in the place. He can't relax; I get nervy; we drive each other remorselessly up the wall."

Frisnay blocked the check with a Rook. He said:

"At least he's found a case that doesn't involve me officially. That's a change."

"I wouldn't bank on that, Freddie. Hugo's expert at involving people, officially or otherwise."

The telephone was ringing. She answered it.

"Hello, Hugo."

"Any message for me?"

"Yes. Miss Levinson rang, about fifteen minutes ago—at ten-thirty-five. Message is: Derek Veiss joined party at Number Three, Hoxton Square, South-West Seven. She has now signed off, as she has to be up crack o' dawn *mañana*."

"Three, Hoxton Square."

"Are you enjoying yourself, Hugo?"

"Vaguely. I met the fat man, then lost him again."

"He must be a past-master."

"Yes. Also an ex-policeman. Very embittered, beneath superficial *bonhomie*."

"How do you know he's an ex-policeman?"

"It's written all over his feet."

He rang off, left the telephone-box, drove down through Chelsea, and stopped to look at his road-book in S.W.7. He was within five minutes of Hoxton Square.

The house was tall, Victorian, half-shuttered; but windows were bright along the top floors. He judged the party to be there.

It was one of those parties where one can walk cheerfully in, ostensibly having returned from the toilet or from a brief *affaire* with the host's younger sister in the linen-closet. It was not the kind of party Bishop liked. A few people were milling gently in the corridor, spilling their drinks and laughing gustily. He assumed a cheerful list to one side and edged carefully into the main room, his face disfigured by a forced smirk so that it would match most of the others.

After ten minutes he learned that there was no host, but a hostess; that the party had started an hour before and was expected to end about dawn; and that those present comprised, among others less talented, two Blues, an Armenian racing-driver, the dispossessed heir to a crumbling pile in County Down, four reefer-smokers, and a nymphomaniac. He had also caught a glimpse of Derek Veiss; and now Veiss saw him, and made his way through the throng. Without formalities the boy said:

"What are you doing here?"

"Enjoying the party. Aren't you?"

He was surprised to find Veiss still sober, but decided that politics and women must absorb his total energies.

"So you did call on my father to talk about Marilyn."

"Did I?"

"What have you told him?" There was no trace of accent, only of heat.

"Not very much," Bishop said. He sipped his cocktail.

"Did you come here with Fenton?"

Blandly, "Is Fenton here?"

"You know he is."

"Well then, you must decide for yourself."

The boy's hands were clenched. He seemed very restive about something. He said with controlled calm:

"I shall. I shall decide a lot of things."

Bishop nodded amiably. "Good man. 'He who hesitates', you know..."

"I shan't hesitate, don't worry."

Bishop felt bored. He murmured, "I'm not actually worrying." He was slowly forming the disheartening idea that this was a wrong track, a time-waster; that the boy had nothing to do with

Jones, with the three prisoners, with anything at all except women and politics. But he was the adopted son of Veiss; and Veiss was interesting.

The boy left him suddenly without another word. In his place a woman was standing, as if there had been a magical transformation. At this party he would not have been very surprised to find a drunken unicorn standing before him in a puff of brimstone.

"Hello, Mr. Bishop."

She was tall, lean-hipped, and tawny-looking. Her nails were lacquered gold. Her voice was like honey being poured through a velvet sieve at sundown. But despite these things, she looked interesting, and she was not tipsy.

He said, "I'm sorry. I'm not often at a loss, but—?"

"We've never met. I just know your name. Mine's Georgina Hutton. Tell me, who was the good-looking boy who was talking to you?"

"Derek Veiss."

"He seemed annoyed with you."

"He was. He thinks I'm someone else, but I don't know whom."

She turned her head. She did this gracefully. It was like a swan wheeling on moonlit water in the shade of willows.

She poured out some more honey. "One of Fenton's friends, possibly?" She turned back to look at his face. He decided to give her some rope.

"Possibly. But I've never met anyone called Fenton. In fact I'm rather at a loss all round."

"Gate-crashers always are. They're bound to be."

He raised one eyebrow. She said, "But don't worry. I'm gate-crashing myself tonight."

"But you know more people here than I do."

She smiled. It was a nice photogenic smile, but Bishop was reminded of opening his refrigerator. She said:

"You know young Veiss. You've heard of Fenton. You've heard of Marilyn—"

"Ah, yes, Marilyn. Now who is she?"

"The girl over there. Our hostess."

He looked across her bare shoulder, with difficulty. Her shoulder was difficult to look across. He saw the girl she meant. That one would be the nymphomaniac. To catch those eyes would be to read the entire Decameron in 3-D Cinecolor.

He said, "That is our hostess?"

"Yes."

"And young Veiss—?"

"Is one of her *affaires*. His people have told him to drop her, but of course he has as much chance of doing that as of coming out of the Inferno alive."

It fitted in. There was Marilyn, the cause of the

disturbance in the Veiss household. And Fenton?

"And Fenton?"

Georgina Hutton said, "Another poor devil in the running, much older than the boy. As I have it, Fenton told Veiss that if he didn't keep away from Marilyn he would approach his parents. Through a friend."

"Through a friend. That would be myself."

"So Derek believes. Hence his annoyance with you."

"I'm getting," Bishop said, "a much clearer picture."

The smile came again, frosting the atmosphere.

"Yes? But so far you've only seen the frame. And not all, even of that."

He tilted his head, watching her. "And you?"

"I've seen all the picture. I'm even in it somewhere, decorating a quiet corner. It's not very pretty. The colors are harsh, daubed in with an almost Spanish violence."

His mind span. He said:

"And the brushwork . . . the execution—?"

"There's no real execution. They fell down on that."

"What are you trying to make me tell you?"

"Anything you can."

"Did you follow me here?"

"I—imagined you'd come."

"Do you know the fat man?"

She hesitated. "The ... fat man?"

"A cheerful chap, rotten underneath with bitterness."

"What size in hats?"

"Did he tell you I'd be here?"

"I don't know any fat man. I prefer my men to be lean."

"You can tell me about—" He broke off. Halfway across the room, Marilyn stood between Derek Veiss and a dapper, clean-cut man with big shoulders and no height. Bishop thought it might be Fenton. He murmured:

"Would that be Fenton?"

"Yes."

They heard Fenton's voice clearly. "Get out, you little fool ... "

"I'll go, if you'll come with me, Fenton." Veiss had his feet astride. He looked as though he wanted to hit someone. Preferably Fenton. Fenton said to the woman:

"Marilyn, I'm sorry about this."

She didn't look as if she were sorry. She looked as if she were enjoying herself. Veiss said:

"Well, are you coming?"

"The longer you stay here," Fenton said more evenly, "the more of a young idiot you'll look. You know where I live, if you want to talk privately."

Astonishingly, Veiss turned away and left the room.

Bishop said quietly, "How white can a face get?"

"True Aryan type. No sense of humor." She straightened her silk stole. "I must be going, too, Mr. Bishop. Will you stay?"

"For a while. I hope we meet again."

The smile had a little warmth. Or it was less cold.

"Do you, really? We will, you know. You're in the picture, too."

He watched her leave. She did not say good night to anyone, nor glance at anyone. Most women realized the value of making their entrance. This one realized that it is with the exit that the best impression can be left. He could still smell her scent, hear her voice, see the soft light on the bare shoulder. He put her down, all the same, as a woman with no mercy and five aces.

He found another drink and decided to stay for an hour longer. Georgina had gone off to intercept young Veiss, for some reason. Marilyn would be here until the party broke up. Fenton would probably be the last to leave, possibly would not leave at all. Veiss might come back. If he did, Georgina might come back too. The fat man might show up. The night was young.

He tried to convince himself, time and again, that he would find another link with the four condemned men, here in a room full of drunks.

7th
MOVE

♜ BISHOP SAT with the tray balanced on his knees. He would have liked to reach for the morning edition, which lay across the foot of the bed, but it would upset the tray. He tried to read the smaller headlines, upside-down, with the light from the window slanting across the surface of the paper and sheening it. He thought one headline read: CHINESE IMPASSE AT E.D.R. BLOCKS HOPES. He thought, as he stirred the coffee, put the cream in and sipped the coffee through the floating cream-film, that most headlines were indecipherable even the right way up.

Miss Gorringe said as she opened the door, "I didn't know you were awake. Where did you get that?"

"Get what?"

"Breakfast."

"Sent down for it. Have some coffee."

She sat on the foot of the bed. "Have you read this?"

"Only upside-down, so far."

She poured some coffee and said, "Nice party last night?"

"Interesting. Not very nice people."

"Stay late?"

"I was one of the last to leave."

"Who was your hostess?"

"Girl called Marilyn Thorburn."

She stirred her coffee. "Found dead," she said.

"Found what?"

"This morning. By her housekeeper."

Bishop put his cup down. "How d'you know?"

"New Scotland Yard rang, about an hour ago. Name of Detective-Inspector Frisnay."

"Is Freddie on the job, then?"

"Yes."

"It's murder?"

"She was shot."

"They found the gun?"

"You'd better ask Freddie."

"Why did he ring here?"

"He knew you'd gone to someone's party last night, because he was here when you phoned for Vic Levinson's message. And your distinguished motor-car was among those standing outside the flat in Hoxton Square, until two o'clock this morning." She added thoughtfully, "I do hope you'll be able to clear yourself."

Bishop said nothing for two minutes. Then, "Shot. Now that surprises me."

"She's not the type to get killed?"

"I'm not surprised she was killed. I'm surprised she was shot. With a gun."

"It's fashionable."

"No, Gorry, it isn't. Jones wasn't shot. The three Spaniards weren't."

"Good grief! You connect this death with the others?"

"By a dozen links. And Freddie's in charge of the enquiry. Cosy."

"Poor Freddie! Last night he was thanking his stars you hadn't involved him in your case."

"I haven't. *I* didn't shoot the woman."

"You'd better go and tell him, before he sends round for you in a plain van."

"Where did he ring from?"

"The dead woman's flat."

"Number?"

"Milbank 2030."

Bishop took up the telephone while Miss Gorringe saved the tray. When he had got through, Bishop said:

"Freddie—Hugo."

"I've been expecting you."

"I thought I'd phone first, to make sure you were there. I'm on my way round. All right?"

"Yes."
"Anything fresh turned up?"
"Yes."
"Give me fifteen minutes."
He hung up.

Frisnay stood with his hands in his jacket pockets, watching the photographers. Another man was measuring from the divan to the door. Two men were dusting for prints. Sergeant Flack was helping a man with the inventory. In five minutes Frisnay said:

"Flack."
"Sir?"
"When Mr. Bishop gets here, I'm not telling him about the autopsy until he's had a look round the place himself. I want to get his reaction."
"All right, sir. Not a word."

Flack stepped over the sheet-covered body and asked for a photograph to be taken from the doorway. He knew Mr. Frisnay always liked to look at a murder-room the way it was when the murderer came in. The pity of it was that they could never take a picture of the body as it had been at that moment, opening the door with a smile or a frown of surprise or a look of terror; or just waiting, idling at the piano or lighting a cigarette; or tying the negligee at the last moment, so that it should fall away slightly as she came to meet him across the room. It would have been interesting, if murderers took pictures, as they came in; interesting to see how people met the last person they would ever meet, strumming a last tune, smoking a last cigarette, dressed intimately for a last hour of love.

Marilyn had merely been drunk.

Frisnay, gazing thoughtfully at her outline under the sheet, felt that it was one of the easier ways out: too drunk to know, to care, to be terrified.

Flack turned and opened the door an inch, hearing the knock. Then he opened it wider, for Bishop to come in. Bishop looked at the room, the sheet. Frisnay came over with his hands still quietly in their pockets.

"Have a good look round."

"Yes," Bishop said. He put his pipe away: Frisnay didn't like pipe-ash all over his circumstantial evidence. He had spent a long time, once, saving a few flakes of pipe-ash and having them compared in the laboratory with other flakes that had been burned in the pipe of a man under suspicion. He had not spoken to Bishop for a week afterwards.

Bishop lifted the end of the sheet and looked at the thing that had been christened Marilyn, tended with loving care, sent to a good school, and launched into its adult life with great hopes. Now there was just this vessel of already-changing chemicals. She'd never be older than thirty; it was every woman's dream.

She was wearing her pyjama-top, nothing else. She had been meaning to get into bed, and had been interrupted. The buttons had not been done up. The bullet had gone in below the left breast, accurately. No powder-burns. Bishop dropped the sheet and looked round the room slowly, keeping out of the way as Frisnay's technical unit worked. Then he came back and said to Frisnay:

"Any sign of the gun?"

"Yes. We picked it up in the basement area, below this window."

"It was the one that fired the bullet?"

"Ballistics are checking now. There weren't any prints."

"Gloves?"

"No," said Frisnay. "The gun was wiped." He went on looking at Bishop. "Well, how does it strike you?"

"I'm disappointed. It looks like a straightforward finish to a demi-rep's career. All you do now is find out which one of the lovers might have been capable of turning a gun on her, and dig up all the mud to sift the evidence."

Frisnay grunted. "You're disappointed. Is that all?"

"What else am I expected to be?"

"I don't know. But you were here last night. You talked to her. You were one of the last people to see her alive."

Flack came over and stood looking down through the window. He was looking at Bishop's car. Bishop said to Frisnay:

"I've no doubt. There were only two people left here when I went. A man called Fenton, and another man whose name I never got; a sugar-daddy from South America, I should say, anxious to bid high for the dolly before his arteries dried up. The only interesting thing that happened at the party was Fenton and young Veiss having a row. Veiss left at about eleven-thirty in a quiet rage."

Frisnay said, "It sounds too obvious, but we're checking on everyone who was known to be here, including the Veiss kid." He rocked on his heels. "I'm disappointed that you're only 'disappointed,' Hugo."

"All right; I'm surprised, as well."

"Surprised? That she was found dead?"

"That she was found shot dead."

"You would have expected her to have died in some other way?"

"I didn't expect her to die at all, but since she

has, I'm surprised it was this way."

Frisnay said, "Are you listening, Sergeant Flack?"

"Yes, sir," Flack said.

"Go on," said Frisnay.

Bishop shrugged. "That's all I can say, Freddie. I admit I was one of the last people who saw her alive, but it doesn't give me any insight into who killed her."

Persisting, Frisnay asked, "How would you have *expected* her to die?"

"Of heart-failure."

Frisnay went on rocking on his feet. He said: "She wasn't shot."

Bishop looked at him and said nothing.

"Our doctor," Frisnay said, "has told us that the bullet went into her dead body. She'd been dead at least five minutes."

"I see," said Bishop.

"And the bullet wouldn't have killed her anyway, because it lodged in a rib."

"And how," Bishop asked without looking at either Flack or Frisnay, "does your doctor say she died?"

"He doesn't know. We've called in the Home Office pathologist."

"He won't diagnose anything startling."

"What makes you think so?"

Bishop half-turned, looking down at the thin

white shroud, thinking how attractive that thing had been last night, how attractive as a female of her species. He said:

"This is the way Jones died. It's the way the Spanish prisoners died."

"But they weren't shot afterwards."

"This death wasn't in public. The others were. She was found just here, on the floor?"

Frisnay nodded. Bishop said:

"Well, how did it go, from your angle?"

"The most likely theory is that whoever came here to shoot her, broke in quietly; or he stayed behind, from the party, in hiding. He saw her there, on the floor, and he thought she was too tired or too drunk to get into bed. So he just fired the gun."

"And was disturbed?"

"Why?"

"The gun," Bishop said, "was found in the basement area."

"You mean if he didn't have to get clear in a hurry, he wouldn't have dropped the gun?"

Bishop said, "I don't mean anything. This is your theory, not mine. I'm just trying to make it fit, because if we don't try very hard, it never will. I think it's about as solid as a fish-net nylon."

Frisnay said reasonably, "All right, better it."

Bishop leaned with his back against the

window-sill, so that he could watch the sheet and imagine Marilyn, and try to imagine what had made her tick, until the spring broke.

"Suppose we say that all these people—Jones, the Spaniards, this woman here—died in the same way. Of the same thing. Suppose it's been murder, all along the line."

"You can't make—"

"Suppose," said Bishop. "For the moment—suppose. Because, you see, this is the same pattern, Freddie, isn't it?"

"Pattern?"

"Jones was going to be hanged. The Spaniards were going to be shot. This girl was also going to be shot—"

"She *was* shot—"

"But only because the man with the gun didn't know she was dead. With the others, it was clear. They fell down. She didn't. This is how the man with the gun saw her. So the pattern is the same. These were all *condemned* people. Marilyn Thorburn was condemned because there was the idea in someone's mind of killing her."

Frisnay folded his arms. "Well?"

"So the shooting would have been in good faith. The bullet was meant to kill."

"I'm with you," Frisnay said.

"But I don't like that theory either," said Bishop.

"Oh, for Pete's sake—"

"Try this one. The shooting was a cover-up. To take away the similarity with the other deaths. Then the gun would have been dropped deliberately, to make the situation obvious: Thorburn had been shot dead, and didn't die like Jones and the Spaniards. Someone wanted to *break* the pattern, to stop you linking this death with the others."

Frisnay said, "Jones wasn't murdered. I don't know about the Madrid affair, but Jones wasn't murdered. I've seen the report of the inquest. There were witnesses—"

"Yes. Dr. Veiss was one of them. And last week he was in Madrid. And last night his adopted son was here, in this room."

"It doesn't make it murder."

Bishop walked across the room, taking his time, to get away from their physical influence. Frisnay and Flack didn't link this body with the others. They were very obstinate about that. Bishop got it clear in his mind, and came back slowly.

"Say this, then. I'll stake a lot on this. If Jones wasn't murdered, neither was this woman. The cause of all these deaths—five of them now—has been the same. That's my theory, and I can support it. It's more credible, I know, that this woman was murdered. Not by the shot, but by some means. And if she was murdered, then Jones was. They all were."

Frisnay began speaking, but the telephone rang and Flack moved; but Frisnay said:

"All right."

He picked up the receiver and said into the mouthpiece:

"Yes?" He held the receiver carefully, and listened carefully. Bishop was beside him, and could hear the voice.

"Who is that?"

Frisnay said, "This is Miss Thorburn's flat. Who's calling, please?"

"Is Miss Thorburn there?"

"She's not available. Can I take a message?"

"What's happened? Is she all right?"

Frisnay looked at Bishop. He said into the phone:

"If you'll give me your name, I'll ask her to telephone you."

"It's nothing important. Thank you."

The line went dead.

Frisnay moved the contact up and down until the Exchange said: "Can I help you?"

"Yes. Police here. Will you please try to trace a call that came through to this number about a minute—"

"Freddie," Bishop said.

"M'm?"

The Exchange was asking what number Frisnay was calling from. Bishop said, "I know who it was."

"Certain?"

"Yes."

Frisnay told the Exchange to cancel that, and hung up.

"Who?"

"Derek Veiss."

"You're certain?"

"Yes. I was talking to him last night." He added thoughtfully, "So he doesn't know she's dead."

"Or he's covering himself—"

"No, he would have given you his name, if that was his purpose."

"Quite true. But he asked if she were 'all right.'"

Bishop said, "He's got a rumor, then."

"Who from?"

"Someone who knows." Bishop was looking at the thin, clean sheet, thinking how hygienic it all looked, and how mucky it really was. "The only one who knows," Bishop said.

Frisnay grunted. Bishop said, looking at him:

"Veiss. Veiss the father. The boy will have spoken to him this morning. Veiss is more cheerful—no longer worried about his foster-son's entanglement—might even drop a hint that the *affaire* is over now. So Derek rings this number, because he wants to know what's happened, or if anything's happened."

After a long time Frisnay said, "Veiss."

"The common-factor. You can't get away from him, can you, Freddie? And what interests me more is: can he get away from you?"

"First, I'll see the boy. Then I'll talk to Veiss."

Bishop nodded, and took his *meerschaum* out. "Yes. You'll crack the boy more easily. Unless he's got less on his mind than Veiss." He filled the white bowl with tobacco. "Then," he said, "you'll crack the man more easily."

"You think Veiss is up to his neck, don't you?"

"I think he's up to his eyebrows." He began wandering towards the door. "Will you let me know how it goes?"

"I will. You're off now?"

"I think so. It's raining hard, and I left the windows of the car open."

"I've heard smarter excuses."

"You don't need me any more, Freddie?" He took out his box of matches.

"No. You're a free man."

Bishop opened the door and looked back and said as an afterthought, "Freddie."

"Yep?"

"When you see old man Veiss, handle with care. I think he's an authority on heart-failure."

Outside the door, he lit his pipe, and left a

thin blue trail behind him down the corridor. This was the corridor where the boy Veiss had walked, in his quiet rage; and where Georgina Hutton had walked, to follow him. Where had they gone? Had they gone together?

He could remember her scent, a light, almost astringent scent that suited her mentally rather than physically. She was a very keen number, Bishop thought—very keen at thinking, and doing it quickly. For all those lush lean looks, there was a brain there, nimble and full of tricks.

He stood on the porch. The rain came down bead-bright and straight, shining on the stones. He stepped off the porch, and went down the steps and across the pavement. He opened the door of his car and Georgina, who was sitting in the back, said, " Hurry, or you'll get wet."

8th MOVE

AND HERE was the scent again, delicate and astringent in the car.

"That's why I did," she said.

"Did what?"

"Got in." He closed the door. "I didn't want to get a soaking. Do you mind?"

"I'm delighted." He tried to put feeling into it. He would have liked time off to think, about Thorburn's death, without anyone talking. That was why he had come away. He said, "Come and sit in the front."

She changed seats and said, "I agree it's more intimate."

He said, "I wasn't thinking about that. It was to save me ricking my neck every time I wanted to look at you."

Her smile cracked, it was so cold. He said, "How did you know this was my car?"

"Only you could own a car like this. More timid mortals wouldn't have the nerve to go about in a mobile Taj Mahal."

He started the engine. After the whirr of the starter had died away, there was no sound of the forty-five horsepower turning over. They might have been sitting alone in a cathedral. It even looked a little like that.

"And how," he asked, "did you know where to find it?"

"I was going to call on Marilyn. You remember, she was our hostess, last night—"

"But of course, now you remind me."

"Then I saw two police-cars outside, and this elegant sedanca, so I thought I'd wait down here for you."

"I see." He did not see.

"As a matter of fact," she said—and he thought she was lying, or going to lie, because "as a matter of fact" was a nervous, self-conscious opening if ever there was one—"I thought you must have left your car outside here all night. Then I realized you might have some connection with Scotland Yard."

He said nothing.

She lit a cigarette. "Tell me, how is Marilyn?"

"Rather quiet, this morning."

"Have the police come to take her away?"

"Eventually."

"What's the charge?"

"I don't think it's a criminal offense to be dead."

Her cigarette-smoke went curling out of the window as she wound the glass down an inch.

"Marilyn Thorburn is dead?" she asked.

"Yes."

"Poor girl, cut off in her prime."

He said, "You don't sound surprised."

"Should I? We all get round to it, once in our lifetime. If you're not booked-up, shall we go and have coffee somewhere?"

His hands rested on the wheel. "If you'd like to."

"Or you could just drop me somewhere dry, if my conversation bores you."

He said, "Where would you like coffee?"

"You decide. But somewhere exceptionally good."

"The Worcester Shades."

"Yes. There."

He moved the clutch, but did not drive off. She said:

"It's an unpleasant subject, over coffee, so I'll ask you now: exactly what happened to Marilyn?"

"She was found shot."

"Do they know who did it?"

"No. Do you?"

She smiled. "No, but I should say the list of

suspects would be pretty long." She added, "What are you waiting for?"

"That taxi."

"Over there? Why?"

"The fat man's in it."

"The fat man?"

"Wherever I go, he goes. He makes me feel quite nervous."

"You mean he follows you about?"

He nodded. "That's right. How often does he report to you—every hour?"

She dropped ash off her cigarette. She said:

"You're dreaming."

"Yes. I'm dreaming that you were just getting into my car when I came out of the house. There was no other taxi in sight, and you didn't come in a private car because these were here when I came; and you didn't walk here, even from the corner, because your clothes are only spotted with rain. So you came in that taxi." He let the clutch in. "I think we can drive off now, without losing him."

They turned the corner. The taxi swung into the mirror. Georgina said in a few minutes:

"Who's the girl?"

"The girl?"

"The pretty one with dark hair."

"Oh. I came back from Madrid with her."

"She followed Derek Veiss to that party last

night, and then phoned your number. That seems quite efficient. But you weren't so successful with Starling."

"Starling. He's fat man?"

"Yes." She threw the cigarette away. "Soon after you lost him, he was behind you, just as he is now. He's very good, isn't he? We're quite proud of old Starling."

"You should be. When did he resign from the police force?"

"He didn't actually resign. After twenty-two years' excellent service he suffered a slight lapse and stole seventeen shillings from a colleague. That's less than a shilling a year, isn't it? They kicked him out, and of course there's no pension."

"They wouldn't have kicked him out. They must have asked him to resign."

"That's true, but he refused. Understandably, he was a little embittered."

"More fool. If he'd resigned, reasonably, he would have kept his pension. Never mind, I'll bet you pay him twice as much."

"He earns it."

They said nothing more until they reached the Worcester Shades. Bishop nosed the Rolls-Royce into a gap big enough to take a bicycle. The big coffee-grinders were turning in the long glass window. She said:

"Wonderful. You can smell it."

They went inside. "Will you order, while I telephone?"

"Yes," he said. "You know where they are?"

"Yes, thank you."

When she came back, she said, "You're very easy to be with, despite the fact that you don't trust me an inch."

"It's a saddening thought, Georgina, that one can only trust the dullest people. You have too much on your mind to be reliable."

"Do you actually hate me?"

"Why should I? You're beautiful, charming, and well-mannered. If you weren't quite so conscious of those things, you'd become human. You'd be really quite a person then. You'd have the world at your feet. At the moment it's at your throat."

Her face was held carefully expressionless. She was less successful with her voice. "I must be easy to read, Hugo."

"Most people are. They want to be. We all think we're the most readable novel in the library."

"You said the world's at my throat. It surprises me that you can sum up my life in a phrase, in an exact phrase."

"There must be others as exact."

She made to answer him, and did not. They drank their coffee, with a silence between them that was neither awkward nor tense. In a measure, he thought it might be possible to like this girl, even to admire her, as a person, rather than as a picture.

"Here comes Major Craddock."

He looked at her in surprise. "Who?"

"Just a friend of mine. I rang him, asking if he'd like to join us here. You don't mind?"

"Of course not—"

"Hello, Charles . . . " Craddock was standing by their table. Bishop looked up.

"My dear Georgina."

A big man, square-faced with a ginger moustache; an ex-Army man with a good handicap, a dull wife, securities, a little blonde comforter in Kensington. Bishop revised the last thought. Craddock was too serious for that, and too inhibited.

"Charles, this is Hugo Bishop—I told you all about him. Hugo—Charles Craddock."

Bishop got up and they found a third chair after each had studied the other for a long second. Bishop said:

"It's nice you're joining us, Major."

Georgina's smile was not cold now. It was a cat's smile; and as Bishop saw its bland satisfaction he knew he had been a fool to let her telephone. She was saying:

"You and Charles have something in common,

Hugo. You're both interested in Dr. Veiss."

"Really?" He studied Craddock again. "And in his work?"

Craddock said, "Especially in his work. He's a brilliant man, as you probably know; and in some ways he's an odd one. His morbid preoccupation with death, for example—you know he went to Madrid recently."

"Yes." Bishop added a characteristic to his picture of Craddock. He didn't waste time talking.

"And then," Craddock said evenly, "he was at Pentonville, of course. And last night his foster-son was at this Thorburn woman's flat. All coincidental, to say the least. We want to find out more about him, you know. That's why we've chosen you as our decoy."

Bishop said carefully, "As your decoy."

Craddock nodded. "You'll be leaving here with us, to a prearranged destination. You'll forgive my directness, I know. We have to work rather quickly, now that Thorburn is dead. You work quickly yourself, Mr. Bishop, so that we should get along very well."

Bishop said, "Are you certain I'll leave here with you?"

"Yes."

"Then, if only on principle, I must refuse."

Stupid, to have let her telephone. Stupid.

She said, "I don't think you will, Hugo."

He said, "I shall be interested, really interested, to see how you—"

A waiter was standing by the table. He glanced up.

"Mr. Bishop, sir?" The waiter looked from Bishop to Craddock and back, undecided.

"Yes?"

"Ah. There's a telephone call for you, sir."

"Thank you."

Craddock got up slowly. He said, "The phone-boxes are near the door. We'll join you, and then go on out, shall we?" He put down some money for the bill. Georgina stood up, taking her bag. They waited for Bishop. He had the unusual, unpleasant feeling of being trapped. But he still couldn't see how they'd do it.

"Yes," he said, and went out of the main room. The waiter was indicating the telephone that stood near the kiosks.

"This one, sir."

"Thank you." He took the receiver, and said, "Hello?"

"Hugo—Gorry."

Craddock was standing a little away, looking through the glass doors at the rain. Georgina was touching up her face. Bishop said:

"Hello, Gorry."

"I'm sorry, Hugo, but I've let you down."

"Have you?"

He still couldn't see—

"There's a man here. I think he's the fat man."

"Yes." So that was how. Too easy. He felt furious, then fought it down. Gorry would be all right. This wasn't her first tight spot. She said:

"I let him in, like a fool—you see—"

"Never mind, don't worry about that. I've just been a fool too. It'll do us good."

She thanked him with a nervous laugh and said, "I let him in because he said he had a message from you. He's now standing over me with a gun. He says he'll shoot to maim unless you go with them. I'm sorry, Hugo."

"It's absolutely all right. But don't provoke him. Tell him I'm going with them. I'll see you soon."

Craddock had turned, and said, "Are you ready?"

Bishop said, "Yes, I'm ready." He said good-bye and put the receiver back.

9th MOVE

THEY STOOD on the pavement, in the steady rain.

Bishop said, "I'll take you in my car, and you can tell me the way."

"Thank you," said Craddock, "but your car is too well known by the police, and we're taking you somewhere private." He opened the door of his Bristol. "Please get into this one."

Bishop looked along the pavement. This might be his last chance, where there were people, where it would be easier to make a sudden disturbance and get clear before Craddock used his gun. His gun was in the pocket of the mackintosh. He was holding it so that Bishop could see it was there.

He got into the car, at the back. It would be interesting to make a shindy and see Craddock worried; but someone might get hurt, some innocent passer-by. And he was even more interested to know as much as he could about Craddock.

"Georgina, will you drive, please? I'll keep Mr. Bishop company at the back."

They got in. She drove off neatly. Bishop, sitting next to Craddock, asked him, "Are you taking me far?"

"Not far. If matters turn out well for you, the return journey won't take long."

"And if matters turn out badly—?"

"There'll be no return journey."

"I see. Well, I enjoyed my coffee. If I'd realized, I would have savored it even more." He looked at the people, the traffic. "What would happen, Major, if I got fed-up, and opened the door, and jumped out?"

"Miss Gorringe would suffer."

"Of course. I wasn't thinking. But how would Starling know I was being unruly?"

"He wouldn't." Craddock took out a packet of cigarettes. Bishop shook his head. "Starling will stay in your flat, facing Miss Gorringe with his gun, until we telephone him and say you have safely reached your destination. He will then leave her, unharmed. Georgina, please drive less fast."

"Sorry."

ROOK'S GAMBIT

"We don't want to attract attention."

"I admire your technique, Major Craddock."

"Thank you, but there's nothing complicated about it, Mr. Bishop."

"No. It's the simplicity I most admire. You've escorted me politely away from a crowded restaurant, against my will, metaphorically coshed and gagged, and are able to tell me that I shan't come back this way unless I'm lucky—and you have complete confidence that I shan't make a move to help myself."

"Your regard for Miss Gorringe is our guarantee."

"Of course. Still, I admire the nerve, the good taste. It's so English in character. Yet I imagine England isn't your country, quite?"

"We are international."

"The world your oyster. How nice, to have so much elbow-room."

The Bristol turned left. Georgina said, "Right, Charles?"

Craddock leaned forward. His hand stayed in the pocket of his mackintosh.

"Second left. The little second-hand bookshop, on the left side. We can park there, without any trouble."

Bishop said, "I expected to be blindfolded before now."

Craddock sat back comfortably. "It would look

unusual, to passers-by. We don't want to attract attention. The owner of the bookshop is away, and we chance to have the keys; so that it wouldn't make any difference if you drew a map of the route. We shan't be there again, after today."

"Neat."

"We can't afford to be untidy. Only a fool leaves litter."

The car was pulled up. Georgina switched off the engine. Craddock said, "You'll come with us, I know, Mr. Bishop, and give no trouble. Remember that until we make the telephone call, Miss Gorringe will be uncomfortable."

"I understand the situation perfectly."

They got out, keeping close to him. Craddock used the keys, opening the shop-door. They went inside. He closed the door.

"Sit down, won't you?"

Bishop saw two chairs, a desk heaped with papers and piles of books. An old velvet jacket hung from a nail at the end of a bookshelf. There was a wastepaper-basket drowned in crumpled sheets of paper. A smell of tobacco, of age, of philosophy.

Bishop leaned against the desk and watched Craddock as he picked up the telephone, saying, "I'll take care of Miss Gorringe for you."

"Thanks. The number is—"

"We know your number." He dialled it. Georgina lit a cigarette, looking at Bishop. He didn't know what the look meant. It wasn't unfriendly; it wasn't intimate. It was over Craddock's head: this look was for Bishop alone. He wondered how strong the relationship was between these two; how deep.

Craddock said into the telephone:

"We have arrived."

He put the receiver back. Bishop said:

"I'm relieved."

"Of course. We're sorry it had to be done; but she'll be left in peace now, to make a cup of tea and relax." He spoke quickly, with an occasional movement of his hand that saved a word here, an explanation there, sometimes an apology. "It will help us if I tell you more about the situation, at this stage. We want to know all we can, about Veiss, and about his work, and why he is involved, so far, in five deaths. I don't know whether you have any firm theory, yet. This is ours. Veiss is a radiophysicist, at present working on television and electrical waves of other kinds. We think he has stumbled upon a means of transmitting electrical energy over a distance, from a small instrument. A kind of shock, effectively influencing living matter, if it is subjected to it. He has, probably, experimented on animals and birds. We might imagine his private excitement, having found in his hands a weapon such as this."

The silence drew out to three seconds, four. Bishop said:

"You can imagine my skepticism."

"Not really." Craddock's head tilted. "You have a good brain. This idea must have occurred to you, as it has to us. You would like to test it. We are testing it now. Just as Veiss came to the inevitable point when he had to test his invention—on a human being."

Georgina was still watching Bishop. He was aware of her eyes. He did not look away from Craddock. "But Veiss," said Craddock, "is not a bad man. He is a naturalized Briton with a love for this country. England has been a generous host to many refugees, during and after the war; and Veiss is a German-Jew. He fled his country to save his life."

Bishop moved, filling his pipe. Craddock watched his hands intently until the tobacco was lighted. "Dr. Veiss is now in a position to take lives himself; as many as he cares to, without penalty, if he is careful. I'm sure there's no one he wishes to murder; but few men, with a weapon like this in their hands, could resist the temptation to test it and find out whether it is as deadly to humans as it is to lesser animals. So his choice was obvious. He needed dying men for his guinea-pigs; men whose death was inevitable. Jones, and the Spanish prisoners."

He took a cigarette from Georgina. Before he lit it, Bishop said:

"Marilyn Thorburn wasn't dying."

Craddock flicked the lighter and said:

"Someone had the idea of killing her. Shooting her. I believe you've been to her flat this morning. Probably you have even seen her body. You are working with the police."

"If you like to think so." He hesitated, then, "I think it would help me, in the same way, if I put you right on certain facts; but of course you may already know them: you're remarkably well-informed. The bullet that was fired at her went into a rib. It didn't kill her."

"Quite so."

Bishop had no means of telling whether Craddock had known this, or whether he was pretending the knowledge. In what way, possibly, could he have known about the bullet in the rib? He took a swerve in the discussion, hoping it might be a short cut. "But where does Dr. Veiss come in?"

"On the heels of the foster-son, Derek. The boy was infatuated with a woman whose influence was the worst imaginable on a young man of his age and background. Dr. Veiss had someone he wished to murder. Someone who was not condemned, as the others were. So he went a step further, passing his own judgment on the woman, condemning her to death, and—after all, how easy. How tempting..."

"Suppose Veiss killed her, then. Who shot the body?"

"Perhaps Veiss himself realized that a fifth unaccountable death might arouse speculation, bring an enquiry, an enquiry of some size, involving all those deaths. So he shot her body, to"—he gave a slow, narrow-eyed smile—"I was about to say: to make it look like murder. You see what I mean, Bishop, about his new power—he can murder so easily that if he wants it to *look like* murder, he must provide false evidence." The smile had gone. He shrugged. "But we're not interested in who shot the body. We want to know, for certain, whether Veiss has a lethal weapon capable of killing at a distance—a weapon, in fact, many times more efficient than the most accurate rifle yet perfected. That is where you come in, as you must realize by now."

The little shop seemed frozen, suddenly, suddenly stilled. It had become, in the last few seconds, a morgue.

"Yes. I realize now."

"I'm sorry," said Craddock, formally.

"Please don't apologize."

"We have nothing personally against you, except that—"

"But of course not. Except that you'd prefer me dead."

Craddock drew on his cigarette. Georgina cleared her throat. Bishop thought: she's not liking this bit much. It's too cold-blooded. He said:

"You're fetching Veiss here?"

"Yes."

"By force?"

"No. We dislike using force—not because it's really the weakest means, but because we prefer co-operation."

"Veiss is to demonstrate here?"

"Yes. A good word. Demonstrate."

"Willingly?"

"Yes."

"And after the demonstration?"

"We shall avail ourselves of the instrument."

"There's also the slight problem of my remains."

Georgina turned away and Bishop heard her cigarette-case snap. He was glad she was nervous. It reassured him, to know that the enemy, or one of the enemy, was nervous. He began feeling better. He said to Craddock:

"You're taking a lot of trouble to get hold of this thing. You must have a good use for it."

"No use at all. We shall offer it for sale. If it can be manufactured easily, I estimate the price of the prototype at roughly a million pounds."

"And the world's your market?"

"Not really. One or two countries won't be invited to the sale. America and Russia will bid high enough to satisfy us."

"You don't mind which?"

"We don't mind which."

Bishop said, "You'd better go and fetch Veiss."

Craddock eyed him obliquely. "It would be kinder, to you." He stubbed out his cigarette. "Georgina, I shall rely on you, completely. Bishop is far from a fool. I expect absolute control while I'm away."

She turned to face him. "Are you talking to a schoolgirl?"

He nodded. "Very well."

They watched him go out, shutting the door. Bishop did not hear the lock snap. He couldn't see whether there was a Yale or not.

He leaned away from the desk, and Georgina said:

"If I let you leave here he'd kill me, out of hand."

"Craddock?"

"Yes."

He said, "I suppose that has a silencer?"

"Yes. You must have seen one before."

"Actually, no. I've never played at cops and robbers before." The thing he didn't like was that she was so nervous. She had no stomach for this. And when they were nervous, they just dragged the trigger back if you sneezed. Now that she was holding the neatly-silenced .23 Kleiger, it wasn't a good thing that she was nervous. He said:

"This is the first time I've been in a bookshop without browsing. It's a bit like being locked in the bathroom with no soap."

"Don't move about, Hugo."

"Sorry." The smoke went up from his pipe, and he realized he was drawing on it too quickly. There were too many nervous people in here. He said:

"As a matter of interest, why should Veiss want to kill me?"

She sat down, slowly, feeling with one hand for the chair behind her, so that she could relax, and rest the silenced barrel of the gun along her thigh. She said in a moment:

"You were at Thorburn's party last night, and saw Derek and Fenton having a scene. Fenton had obviously cut the boy out, as regards Marilyn. So Derek decided that no one should ever have her."

"Not madly original."

"Is lust?"

"Point conceded."

"After Derek left the party he stayed near the house, and came back later. You saw him. You are ready to inform the police. You are working with them. We can't stop you. Veiss can."

She looked lovely, sitting there. She looked like a child, only just grown up. If he gave her a new ribbon for her lovely hair, would she . . . ? No. Appearances lied. She was a mean-gutted little alley-cat with dirt in her claws. He had to remember that. But it was difficult. In choosing this woman for a partner, Craddock had been subtle. This lithe Venus with eyes like heaven-on-earth was better than a bruiser with arms like saplings. So long as she had the gun.

He said, "That is the story you're telling Veiss?"

"Yes."

"But he might believe me, when I deny it—"

"He can't risk it."

"But even if I told the police I actually saw the boy fire the gun, he wouldn't be charged with murder. That gun never killed."

"He'd be involved, seriously, in a murder case. It would bring the limelight on Veiss. Veiss wants to keep in the dark."

"The shy type."

She said, "I like your nerve, Hugo."

He said, "I wouldn't sell it for a pension. I suppose it doesn't worry Veiss that after he's given his little demonstration the limelight is liable to flare up. A sixth death, in circumstances—"

"It won't be murder. You'll die of heart-failure."

"Yes, of course. This season's fashionable disease. I wonder how it feels."

"I hope it's painless." She spoke thickly. Her eyes were trying to look away from him. He wondered if the door had a Yale. Craddock hadn't turned a key, going out. He had used a key, coming in. She looked lovely, sitting there, but he must remember the dirt in the claws. She swallowed and said, "I hope it won't have to end like that. If Veiss shows the weapon before he—he uses it, we'll try to take it from him, in time. We don't like wanton killing."

Slowly he said, "In your job, you must be faced, sometimes, with unpleasant necessities."

She looked down, but watched his hands.

"Now and then I have to go through with something that I wish I'd never started. But don't imagine I'm turning soft at the core, Hugo."

"Turning human?"

"Not even that." She raised her eyes. They looked like hard blue stones. "I wasn't born into your kind of world. I've never learned your set of values. When I was six, my father, was sentenced to life-imprisonment by a political tribunal; but it wasn't a long sentence. He lived two years more." Her voice began running over rough gravel. "My mother was tortured into insanity before she could find a way out of our country. I got out, before I was fifteen, by killing a man in cold blood. He was naked. He thought I was going to let him play with me. I've always remembered the blood. It looked as if he was wearing something striped. Red and white stripes, and—" She stopped, and slowly moved the gun from her right hand to her left, relaxing her right hand, hanging it limply across the arm of the chair.

Deliberately he said, "You've worked out the sob-story technique to a fine art."

She said, "But just because those were my formative years, it doesn't give me any excuse to be inhuman. There were thousands like me, before the war and during it, all over Europe. The English don't know much about Europe; it's their insularity. They've never had pogroms, purges, things like that. But in some countries there were a lot like me. Some of us went mad or killed ourselves or shut ourselves away—there are many still in asylums, in convents. But I've got claustrophobia and I don't believe in God. I believe in two things."

"Life and death."

"How well you always hit the mark. It makes me scared of you."

"I haven't the gun."

As if she had just remembered it, she moved it, training the long muzzle at his chest. She said,

"My philosophy is very simple, now. I mean to live till I die."

"You haven't had any time to think of any—"

"If I'd had time to think, I'd be a lunatic or a suicide or a nun. Thoughts can turn bad in the brain."

His pipe had gone out. He lit it, watching her face. Her eyes were on his hands as they moved; the pupils were large. She would have pressed that thing automatically if he had taken one step towards her, suddenly. He said:

"I see things more clearly now. My death is going to be just another."

"No, not quite. I haven't met anyone before—any man, I mean—who can get under the skin so—so efficiently as you."

He said, "That makes me sound like a hypodermic syringe."

"You find my sentiments amusing—"

"Just out of tune with the moment. You couldn't leave any man cold, Georgina; but today you don't look your best. A beautiful woman is badly dressed holding a gun."

She watched him with her eyes widening, as she thought of what she was going to say. "If you gave me your word, I'd put my gun down."

"My word?"

"To stay here until they come."

"You'd take my word, alone?"

"Yes."

"I wouldn't keep it. My life's at stake."

"Then you wouldn't give it."

He smiled. "No. I wouldn't. It's tempting, but..." The smile went. His eyes became as hard as hers. "Georgina, keep the gun steady, and watch me every second. I mean to leave here alive, even if it entails killing you. This is just a fair warning. I wouldn't break my word, but if I can, I'll break your neck."

He thought: if I offer her a ribbon, for her lovely hair; a thousand-pound ribbon, just to make her smell money; then give her the other thing she wants, turn her over to Gorry, teach her kindness, goodness, give her the faith she needs, the faith she'll die without, soon, the faith in ordinary people, in herself... would it work?

"It would be nice," he said, "to try turning you into a young woman."

"What am I now?"

"An alley-cat."

Her mouth lost its shape.

"It would be nice to show you the other side."

"How smug can you get?"

"You might die without ever having seen the other side."

"I'm reduced to tears."

"You'll never cry. It's human, to cry."

"Why are you provoking me?"

He shook his head. "I'm not. I'm talking to you just as it comes, out of my mind. A man near death can say what he thinks, at last."

"You're not that much interested in me."

"Why shouldn't I be?"

"Because I'm—I'm—"

"An alley-cat."

"Yes." The hardness had gone from the eyes, the voice.

He thought it might be possible, one day, to reclaim this one. It was always worth trying. He and Gorry had done it, sometimes, successfully. It was a purely selfish indulgence; to claim a human back from the muck-heap was a satisfying triumph, greater in a way than Pygmalion's. This one could be a walkover; she was young.

"How old are you?" he asked her.

She smiled. "Old enough to shoot."

"That's awfully young." He caught another glimpse of the feather. It was a long green feather that had gone bobbing by, on the other side of the glass panel over the door of the shop. Now it was back.

"You turn hard and soft, Hugo, by numbers. To me you're more dangerous when you're soft."

"It would have been nice, wouldn't it, if we'd met in some other way?" The feather was stationary. It must be a tall one, or the hat must be tall, or the woman; because he hadn't seen other people going past the shop-door, even the hats of tall men. Which book, in the window, would the woman be looking at? Was it an imperious, impervious feather, eager for adventure in lands large enough to accommodate it? *Down the Amazon with Captain Cannon?* Or was the feather there to give height, to make up for timidity, to provide an impressive elongated ego with which to face the world? *How to Live without Fear?* Or was the feather a mere extravagant adornment, a projection of a luxurious lascivious soul? *I Was a Bedouin Bride?*

It moved again. He was fascinated.

Georgina said:

"What are you looking at?"

He said, "You'd never believe it."

She smiled. The icy one. "You're pulling an awfully old trick, Hugo."

"That's right. Trying to make you look round."

The feather trembled.

He said cosily, "Don't worry. It's only a customer—"

"A cu—"

The bell rang over the door as the door was opened. She spun out of the chair and reached the door with the gun held behind her and her voice grating as she tried to get the panic out of it and make it sound normal—"We're closed—I'm sorry, we're closed—"

"We're stock-taking," said Bishop. He smiled politely, over Georgina's shoulder. He could hear her breath scrape in her throat as he brought the pressure on hard enough to block the artery in her wrist. The woman was looking from one to the other, her small bird-like eyes bright with surprise.

"But I wanted—"

"There's a notice," said Bishop, "on the door. It says 'Closed'."

The woman gave a pert little hop, and craned her neck to look.

"Of course there is! And I never saw it!" Her voice floated, chirruping, over her shoulder as she hurried away in confusion. "So sorry ... so sorry ..."

Bishop lifted his right leg and pushed the door shut with his foot. Absurdly, at the back of his mind, right away behind the enormous relief, he thought: she didn't want a book about anything at all. She wears that feather because she's a bird all over.

Georgina was trying to say something. Something that sounded like, "for God's sake..." coming raw out of her throat. They were still together, standing together, he behind her, as a fond lover surprising her for fun, pressing the little jewel-box, her new present, into her hand. "Hugo—"

The gun fell at last and he picked it up, releasing her wrist. she She stood there swaying. Her hand was blue, swollen. He said:

"Rub it." He put the gun into his pocket. "Get the circulation back."

She was mumbling. "He'll kill me, he'll kill me."

He took up the telephone. "It was his fault, you know. He didn't lock the door. He'd be a fool, to blame you."

She was leaning against the shelves, watching him. Her face was clammy. "Are you phoning the police?"

"No." He finished dialling. "You're quite free to go, Georgina. I'm only keeping this thing because I like to know where it is." The line opened.

"Hello?" Voice a little worried. He said:

"Hello, Gorry. The fat man gone?"

"Yes. Are you all right?"

"Yes, thanks. He didn't annoy you?"

A few seconds, before she said, "No. He was very polite. Hugo, I thought you were—?"

"Oh. no. No trouble. I'm on my way home."

He put the receiver down.

Georgina had not moved. She looked very upset, in a quiet white-faced way. He said:

"If you want to be sick, there's a door at the back."

He looked at her, taking his time. He thought it

was probably true, about her mother, her father, the other things. She would have looked like this, then, as a child. She was only a child now.

He stopped, on his way to the door.

"Share my cab?"

She leaned limply. He thought it was probably the pain in her wrist, more than her fear of Craddock and her fury at losing, that made her look like this. Her hand was very thick, the blue skin reddening as the blood cleared slowly.

She looked up at him, as if she had only just registered what he had said. Her mouth moved slackly, telling him he was a bastard. She was running true to type, but at least he admired her spirit.

"Well, I'll be getting along."

He opened the door.

"Hugo—"

"I'm sorry, but I really must go. You've got some people coming, I know."

The rain was still coming down as he walked along the street. It was cool on his face. It was nice to feel.

10th MOVE

"HE RANG me, ten minutes ago."

"Where from?"

"I don't know. The main thing is, he's all right."

Frisnay said quietly, "You must have been worried."

She smiled. "For a time. Can you wait a few minutes, until he comes?"

"Yes." He looked round. He said, "You've been quick."

Bishop came in and shut the door and said, "I was born in the rush-hour." He looked once at Miss Gorringe. She said nothing. It was good to see him, coming into this room again.

"Been waiting long, Freddie?"

"Two minutes. Gorry phoned my office, but of course we couldn't do anything—"

"Didn't know the address, did you? Never mind."

"Hugo." Miss Gorringe was looking at him as he took the .25 from his pocket. "What have you got there?"

"This? Oh—gun."

"Well, do put it down. It looks germy."

He gave it to Frisnay. "Here you are. Lost-property department, though I doubt if it'll be claimed."

"Whose is it?" Frisnay put it away.

"Belongs to the girl-friend. I left her in a second-hand bookshop in Denison Street thumbing through a pamphlet entitled *Are You Frustrated?*" He waved the decanter. "Drink?"

"No, thanks."

"I'm having a Scotch. Gorry?"

"No. I had brandy, after you'd phoned."

He grinned faintly. He took a draught and looked at Frisnay. "You got a line on anything, Freddie?"

"Enquiries are going ahead."

"Ah, the mills of God. Have you talked to Dr. Veiss?"

"Not yet. His wife says he's out."

"Phone Connaught 4346."

"Where's that?"

"Second-hand bookshop in Denison Street."

Frisnay looked patient. "Tell me," he said.

Bishop stood with his tumbler tilted. He watched the liquor clinging. He said, "There are two people. Major Charles Craddock, and Georgina Hutton. Both stateless but not witless. They think Veiss has perfected some kind of weapon that—"

"Ah."

Bishop glanced up. "What d'you mean—ah?"

"Mine isn't the only department interested in the Thorburn killing. The Special Branch is coming in."

"Is—that—so?"

Miss Gorringe was looking at Frisnay. She said, "So this thing has come into the category of affecting the security of the State?"

"Just that. It's my job to find out if it's liable to go that far. If it does, then they take over the background work. They want to know, first, who killed Thorburn."

Bishop finished his whisky. "Don't we all?"

"You say Veiss is at this bookshop. Who with?"

"Georgina Hutton and Craddock. You see, Freddie, we're all working along the same lines—you, me, and these two characters. We're all focused on Veiss. I don't know about you, but we others believe he's actually got such a weapon as would interest the Special Branch. We believe he's killed five people with it already: Jones, the three Spaniards, and Marilyn Thorburn. I personally believe he's reaching the stage where he doesn't know where to stop. I myself have lately become prone to ... heart-failure."

"You? Why?"

"Those two have told Veiss I'm prepared to give you evidence that Derek killed Thorburn. Up to a point I could certainly give you circumstantial evidence—his row with the man Fenton, over Thorburn—but they've cooked up some more, to convince Veiss. They want to drive him into the open, make him use this thing of his—"

"To get a hold on him?"

"To get the weapon. That's all they want. Within a couple of hours you wouldn't find them anywhere in England, once it was in their hands."

"They couldn't convince Veiss easily: unless either he or the boy shot at Thorburn's body."

"Quite."

Frisnay said, "What was the number?"

"Connaught 4346."

"Can I?"

"Do."

Frisnay went across to the telephone and began dialling. Miss Gorringe said quietly to Bishop, "I tried to follow the fat man when he left here, but I lost him. I hoped he might have led me to where you were."

"He wouldn't have. He's impossible to follow."

"You're right about him. He's an ex-policeman. He's still got some of the slang."

"They sacked him, for theft. He's very—"

"Just a minute," Frisnay murmured.

Bishop stood close to him. "They answered?"

"M'm. They've taken the receiver off. Now they're just listening."

"Ask for the foreman tripe-dresser, make them think it's a wrong number."

Frisnay grunted, took his hand away from the mouth-piece and said, "Hello?"

"Yes?" A man's voice.

"Are you Connaught 4346?"

"Who are you wanting?"

"Dr. Veiss. I believe he's there."

"I'm sorry, you've mistaken the number."

The line went dead. Frisnay put the receiver down. Bishop said, "That was Craddock."

"Yes? Still there, then."

He picked up the receiver again and dialled. "The winning treble," he said. The Exchange put him through.

"Police. Can we help you?"

"Inspector Frisnay here. A man, or two men and a woman, at number—"

"Thirty-four, Denison Street," murmured Bishop.

"Thirty-four, Denison Street. Second-hand bookshop. If lucky, hold them till I reach there."

The man at Operations repeated. Bishop said:

"Freddie. Using black Bristol saloon—"

"Number?"

"Never saw it—"

"Might get away," said Frisnay into the phone, "in a black Bristol saloon. Tell them hurry."

"To hurry, sir."

Frisnay hung up. Bishop said:

"What charge?"

"Holding you against your will. Confirm?"

"Yes, but don't go off at half-cock, Freddie. You've nothing else on them yet."

"They're moving quick. As quick as Veiss— Jones died in Pentonville only two days ago— Thorburn was found dead this morning—and you're prone to heart-failure now. Even the mills of God have got another gear."

Bishop picked up a chessman from the board, put it down, thought about Marilyn Thorburn, and said, "Who have you seen, so far, about Thorburn?"

"Half a dozen guests who were at the party. Man called Fenton seems to have it in for Derek Veiss—"

"Does he think Derek had anything to do with it?"

"He didn't say as much. He was very upset. Said Marilyn was the most wonderful woman in the world."

"I think that's putting it a bit high."

"He's keen to know who killed her."

"That's a popular Quiz."

"Well, there's an answer." He found his gloves. "How far's Denison Street?"

"Ten minutes."

"I'll get along down there. They should have had time to—"

The doorbell rang. Miss Gorringe said, "All right."

Bishop said, "You want me to go with you, to identify them formally?"

"Yes, and make a charge." He turned as Miss Gorringe came back. Sergeant Flack was with her. Flack said:

"Excuse me, sir. Call just come through to our car from JK-6. There's no one at Thirty-four Denison Street, and no sign of the Bristol saloon."

Frisnay bunched his shoulders. "Well then, next time. We'll go and see Veiss. I imagine they'll be taking him back, Hugo?"

"Taking him back, or bringing him here."

"Here? What for?"

"Well. Veiss thinks I'm just about to kick the ground from under him. They want to see me again, those three. Alone. It's quite embarrassing, to be so much sought-after."

Before he went, Frisnay said, "You want me to leave a man here?"

"No, thanks. It might frighten the neighbors."

"If Veiss comes here, give us the signal."
"I will, if I see him first."

Vic Levinson rang just before nine that evening. She said she was on the job. Bishop said:

"What job?"

"The Thorburn murder. Our crime reporter, such as he is, has passed out, dead-drunk."

"What was he celebrating?"

"My having bought him a bottle of Scotch. I'm now looking after his column, in a friendly way."

"Ah. And you want copy, official."

"Yes, but not at second-hand, just supposing you wanted to give me anything. I'm trying to pick up the live stuff."

He gazed solemnly at Chu Yi-Hsin, who was perched on his desk gazing solemnly back. He said:

"Where are you, Vic?"

"In a café. I've been here an hour. You drink tea, ever?"

"What's it made of?"

"I can't leave here yet. So I thought if I just rang you, there might be a chance you'd remember my name, and take a moment to come and cheer up a poor working-girl whose face may be plain but whose heart is—"

"I've missed you," he said.

"You have?"

"Where's the café?"

"Called Elsa's. A good pull-up for visiting Bishops. It's at the bottom of Hampstead Lane West. It'll be wonderful to see you again. I'll arrange a secluded table for two—you like to sit facing the tea-urn or the sink?"

He said he would be there, and rang off. The Siamese was watching him. So was Miss Gorringe. She said, "Going out?"

"We both are. I'm dropping you somewhere ritzy, while I slum it in Hampstead—"

"I'll be all right, Hugo."

"You weren't all right when the fat man called."

"Next time I'll be ready. Miss Gorringe is only surprised once during a given period. Other times she turns proper nasty."

He hesitated. "Certain?"

"Sure-fire certain. Has Vic got a lead?"

"It sounds like it. She wouldn't have rung up just to suggest a cup of tea."

He got a mackintosh and went down the stairs to the mews. His car was five paces away. He took three paces, broke his stride, then carried on, opening the driving-door and saying:

"Persistent, aren't you?"

Georgina said, "I'll get out, if you're driving anywhere private."

She looked numbed, still, a little. He got into the car and said, "Have you come to collect your gun?"

"I'm not very good with it, am I? Your car's a good place to keep watch from, in the dark."

"It's also rainproof. Watching for anyone special?"

"Craddock. Or Veiss."

"Or both."

"And if they'd come?"

"I'd have warned you."

"How?"

"Blowing the horns."

"Why?"

"I don't want you killed."

"You've changed."

"Perhaps."

"There's been a split?"

"Yes. Craddock has cut me out. I've proved unreliable."

"Where d'you go from here?"

"Solo. To beat him to it, if I can."

"To get hold of the Veiss instrument?"

"Yes. I wanted you to know, in case Craddock tries to use me against you. It would be against my will."

Bishop lit his pipe and looked down the dim perspective of the mews. The rain sent a gleam of light across the cobble-stones, catching it from the lamp at the end. He said:

"This must be a complicated kind of trap. I can't quite figure out the mechanism yet."

"There's no trap. That's all I came to tell you— that I'm no longer with Craddock."

He said, "I wonder which I should congratulate more?"

She said nothing. He had taken a good look at those corners of the mews that he could see, in the faint light. He thought it would be all right to drive away. He said:

"Where can I drop you?"

"As near as you're going to Hyde Park Corner."

A busy, public place. That would be all right. It was restaurants and bookshops he'd become bored with. He let in the gears.

They cleared the mews and by Sloane Square he was inclined to think it hadn't been any kind of trap, after all.

She was sitting in a corner, with a cup of tea. With her seventh cup of tea. The boy came up with a sniff and a perky look. He said conspiratorially, wiping a quiff of hair back with a deft hand:

"Your name Miss Levinson, is it?"

"That's right."

"Ah. There's a gent outside, wants to see you."

"A gent?"

"Ye'. Out there in a big gray car. Tol' me to keep it quiet, see?"

"Yes, I see. Thank you."

"You're welcome."

She stayed another five minutes, and then went out, with time obviously on her hands. Crossing the road she found the sedanca and said through the driver's window:

" 'Lo, Hugo."

"I didn't come in, because Derek Veiss is sitting in there."

"I know, but he wouldn't have seen you." She touched his hand, on the door-ledge. Their hands rested together. "He's been sitting in there for an hour, staring at the wall. I followed him when he left the University. He started for home, then changed his mind, and walked all the way up here, as if he had time to burn. I think he's waiting for someone."

Bishop said, "No."

She half-turned. Derek Veiss was leaving. Bishop said:

"Get into the car. Quick."

"It's all right, he's turning the other way. I'm wrong. He wasn't waiting for anyone."

"He was killing time."

"But why?"

Bishop said, "The technical station's in this

area—the place where Veiss works."

"That's where he's making for now?"

"Is there a better guess, at short notice?"

The boy went out of sight, into an alley fifty yards down the road. Bishop said:

"We can't follow him down the alley. You can't follow anyone down an alley, unless he's drunk or deaf. Get in."

She climbed in beside him. He said, "I'll drive round the corner, then we can go on foot."

They turned twice, reaching the road that went by the other end of the alley. Vic said:

"There."

"Yes."

"Crossing the road—"

"We'll leave the car here."

They got out quietly. In a moment, Bishop said:

"Over this fence. Can you make it?"

"Yes."

He helped her. Their feet scraped a little, as little as they could manage. The glow of the street-lamp shone across them as they topped the fence; then they dropped into gloom.

She whispered, "Is this the technical station?"

"The grounds. Buildings are over there."

"Can you see him?"

"Yes. He dropped over, some way down."

She moved. She said: "We'll have to take care.

There's gravel here. Some sort of path, that—"

"Vic." He said it very softly, just on his breath.

"Yes?"

"Keep dead still. There's someone else here."

He found her hand. It was cold. She breathed, "Someone else? Where?"

"By the bushes, over that way. Relax your muscles. We'll wait till he moves first."

Rain was soft on the leaves.

Her voice was soft as the rain. "Has he seen us?"

"Yes. He knows we're here."

11th
MOVE

THERE WAS only the sound of the rain, and the faint murmur of traffic in the distance. Minutes had gone by. Her hand was still cold. Her breath came, close to his ear.

"Has he gone?"

"No."

"Can he see us?"

"No. He's waiting for us to move."

"Can you think who it is?"

"It might be anyone. A night-guard, anyone."

"A guard would challenge us."

"Yes. That's why I think it's someone else. Vic, don't move."

His hand groped, gingerly. She murmured, "What are you going to do?"

"Throw a piece of gravel at the fence. He might think we're still over there, where we dropped. Don't let it startle you, when I open the bowling."

He found a small flint. It went scattering along the fence. There was a two-second silence; then a soft, unpleasant thud.

"What was that?"

"A cat."

She started speaking again but he stopped her.

"Keep still, Vic." They were on gravel. He was worried now. The cat must have been perched on the fence. He hadn't seen it, until the flint had struck along the timber. Then the cat had bobbed up. Two seconds later there had been the soft, ugly thud. That was the cat. It hadn't jumped down from the fence. It had fallen, as if shot. But there hadn't been any shot. He was certain, with a feeling of cold in his stomach, that the cat was there, dead.

"Vic."

"Yes?"

"On our left there's a lawn, then the wing of the building. This path isn't wide. When I say, try to reach the edge of the grass in one jump. Then run hard for the cover of the building."

"Yes."

He tried to keep his whisper natural.

"Vic, do it well. It's important. Run hard."

He found three or four chips of stone, and lobbed them high. As they struck the leaves of the bushes he dug her with his fist and said, "Now."

She sprang away from him. He didn't hear her feet on gravel. She had made it in one jump. He followed. The airstream was in his ears. He could see her, dimly, a few yards ahead. He kept close, running low. Half-way across the lawn he caught her up and she said something, but he told her to run, just keep on running. The dark outlines of the building came up and towered over them and they stopped, holding themselves flat against the wall. Her breath was scraping.

"We did it."

"Yes," he said.

"He's not armed. He would have fired, at random."

"That's right. But we're not clear yet. Vic, this is a bad spot we're in—"

"But if he hasn't got a gun—"

"A bad spot. Believe me. Do everything I tell you."

"Yes, Hugo."

A sound came, somewhere along the building. He said:

"Stay here. Just here."

"What was it?"

"I'll be back. Don't leave here. I want to know where to find you."

He left her. It took him five minutes to go twelve yards, because there were obstacles. The coal-bunkers were along this wing, and there was rubbish about. He had to feel every tin can with his foot as a cat sniffs a motor-tire, before he could get through in silence.

The boy was half-way between the ground and a window, standing on a crate. Bishop span him down before he could make any noise and lay on top of him, pinning him. The boy was strong. Bishop had to chop him gently before he would stop struggling. Then he said very softly:

"Don't make a sound when I take my hand away. If you do, you'll get us both killed. I'm going to give you a minute to think that over. You'll get us both killed." He waited. He felt Derek moving his head, trying to nod it. He wished there were time to take more precautions. There simply was not. He took his hand away from the boy's mouth. The boy murmured:

"Who are you?"

"Bishop. Listen. If you stay in these grounds you won't live. Nor will I. So I'm taking you with me—"

"Where?"

"Just out of here. Once we're clear you can go where you like—"

"No. I'm not leaving—"

"Then I'll take you—"

"How?"

"Slug you and drag you."

"I—"

"There's not time. I'm not getting killed, and I'm not leaving you here for dead. I'll give you one more second—"

"I'll come."

Bishop stood up. He was ready to hit the boy down hard if he looked like being silly.

"This way. Keep very close, and no noise, if you want to live."

Vic had not moved. She was crouched by the wall, and caught her breath as Bishop came on her out of the gloom.

"Who's with you?"

"Derek Veiss. Now listen. We're all getting out. Veiss, we're not armed. There's a man in these grounds who is. He knows we're here. He's watching for us now. He's a crack shot. Shall I repeat any of that?"

Derek said softly, "I'll do as you say."

"Good. Walk exactly where I walk. If I stop, stop. If I say run, I'll mean run. For your life."

It took twenty minutes to locate the car, because they had left the grounds on the far side, and the area was a network of alleys and small streets. The rain was easing; above them a few stars winked. Bishop said:

"Veiss, can we drop you near your home?"

"I'd like to talk to you."

"Get in, then. We can talk in the car."

He started the engine. Vic sat in front. Derek leaned against the seats, between them.

"I'd like to ask you—"

"We'll clear this locality before we talk. The neighborhood's unhealthy." He said to Vic: "Have you somewhere to go?"

"No. Can I stick?"

"I'd like you to."

They drove a mile before he said: "All right, Veiss. You can ask me anything you like, but the answers aren't fully guaranteed."

"Who was the man in the grounds?"

"I'm not certain—"

"But you must know—"

"Yes, I know. But I'm not certain. Some of the time we were being fired on. But he missed. Does that mean anything to you?"

"I didn't hear any shots."

"Then it doesn't mean anything to you. Just take my word for it. Question Two?"

"Who killed Marilyn?"

"The man who was in the grounds just now."

The boy's tone went tense.

"Tell me his name."

"No. You might do something rash—"

"I must know who killed her—"

"Then think of someone."

"I've tried."

"Who did you think of?"

"There were people who were afraid of her."

"And now they're not. You think that was the motive?"

Veiss said, "If you know the man, you must know his motive. Please tell me his name."

"I'm not certain." He took out his *meerschaum* and his tobacco-pouch, and passed them to Vic. "D'you think you could fill that, while I'm driving?"

"I'll try, Hugo."

He said to the boy, "It would do a lot of harm if I told you. Why were you trying to break into the technical station? Your father works there, doesn't he?"

"Yes."

"Then why?"

After a moment: "There's a diary, belonging to me."

Bishop thought: that clicks home; that fits. He said:

"A diary. With Marilyn's name on every page—"

"We're not talking about her now." He said it through his teeth. Bishop waited, then said:

"Your father took the diary, and you want it back. It's very private, and now it's become almost sacred to you. What makes you imagine it's at the technical station?"

"There is a safe there."

"With other things in it. Apart from the diary."

Derek was silent. Bishop said, "Various papers. Possibly technical data, references, formulæ."

"I've seen certain papers—"

"You're prying into your father's work, about as hard as you can go. You two don't like each other much, do you?"

"He's not—" Then he shut down.

"Go on talking, if you want me to find out, for certain, who killed her."

"I—I don't understand them, these papers. They're very technical—"

"Is there a name, a title, a subject-heading?"

"They deal with some form of radio-wave transmitter. It's referred to as Z.69."

Bishop turned down towards Tottenham Court Road. The traffic was light; people were eating, drinking, seeing a show. He drove quickly, because he was thinking quickly.

He said, "The Z.69. Have you seen it, ever?"

"No. He's very careful."

"These papers—you had to look for them, hard—"

"I came on them, some of them—"

"Keep any?"

"No—"

"Wise of you—"

"Why are you interested in them?"

"They've a bearing on Marilyn's death."

"Tell me who it was. I've told you everything I can."

"It wasn't enough. What I could tell you wouldn't be enough either, without confirmation." He pulled the car in to a side-street. "This is going to take you out of your way, if you're thinking of going home."

"I'll do anything, if you'll tell me who killed—"

"There's nothing you can do that would help anybody. But you'll have to remember one thing: if you try breaking into that research-station again, you'll be risking your life, every time. There's no reason for me to say that, except for your own good. You can believe me, or not. But I hope you do."

"But why—?"

"Never mind why. Just remember."

The boy got out of the car. He seemed unsure of himself, of Bishop, of where he must go next. Bishop felt sorry for him. He was still a kid. He said:

"Will you be all right now?"

"Yes. Yes, thank you."

He said good night. Bishop drove off, threading back into Charing Cross Road. Vic said:

"Where now?"

"Back to the technical station. Something I want to make certain of."

"You're not going into the grounds again?"
"Yes—"
"But Hugo—"
"I'll take precautions this time—"
"But, darling, I can't let you—" Her voice trailed off.

He said gently, "You can help me."

Small-toned, she said, "I can?"

In the road where they had left the car before there was a telephone-box. He had remembered seeing it. He pulled up alongside it. Its light sent the grille-pattern of the panels across the pavement.

"This must be the nearest one to the grounds. Have you got three coppers?"

She looked in her bag.

"Two."

He found a third from his pocket. He said:

"I want you to ring the technical station. I think that was Dr. Veiss, in the grounds. It's an even chance he's gone into the building, either because he was in there before, when we went crowding over the fence, or because he'll want to check up all round, now that he knows someone was trying to break in. That man is nervous. He's sitting on quite an egg."

She shot out of the car and said through the window:

"If he answers, what shall I say?"

"Anything. Just keep him on the line, while I take a quick look round the grounds, inside the fence. Then I shall know I'm safe."

She looked doubtful. He said, "I only need three or four minutes."

"All right."

"I'm going to drive down this road, fast, the moment I know you've got Veiss on the line. It'll save time. I want to go over the fence in the same spot. Then I'll come back and pick you up. You know the name?"

"Kingston-Electric."

"That's right. When you're through, and talking to Veiss, just nod your head or lift your hand. I'll be watching. But make sure it's Veiss. Anyone else won't do."

She walked across the pavement into the glow of light. The door of the kiosk closed slowly against its air-stop. He put the gears into mesh and sat waiting, with the clutch out. He heard the coppers ring into the coin-box. When she lifted her hand he brought the clutch in and drove away hard.

12th
MOVE

FRISNAY SAT with the receiver held to one ear, his hand to the other. Fresh air was coming through the window; yesterday it had rained from breakfast to evening and the window had been shut. Now it could be opened. It let in the sweet Spring air, and the din of the traffic, muffled by his hand.

He said, "No." He listened and said, "Yes. Find out everything you can about Veiss. What group was he in before the war, in his own country? Ever been convicted of anything, however small? What case did he present when he asked for naturalization? Find out what newspaper he takes, what clubs he belongs to, what organizations he subscribes to. And find out anything we might, if necessary, be able to trip him on, however minor. Has he got a wireless license, a dog license, a car license?—Does he owe any bills? I want everything." He listened again and said, "All right." He put the receiver down and unblocked his free ear. The interphone buzzed. He put the switch down. "Yes?"

"Mr. Bishop's here, sir."

"I'll see him."

He lit another cigarette. Bishop came in.

"Morning, Cock."

Frisnay grunted. He said, "What's that?"

Bishop put the brown-paper parcel on the desk.

"A little gift for Mother's Day."

Frisnay looked patient. He was not feeling patient.

"What's inside?" he asked evenly.

"A stiff puss."

"A what?"

"A dead cat."

Frisnay looked at the parcel, wooden-faced. "It's just what I wanted," he said. He unwrapped the paper and looked at the cat's body. "What d'you want me to do—stuff it?"

"Have it examined." Bishop sat down near the desk. "I think it died of the same thing that Marilyn Thornburn died of, but you might like to have it confirmed."

Frisnay's face looked like the bottom of a cigar-box. He moved his hand, pressing a bell. He said:

"What's the story?"

"Last night I found myself in a slight fix—"

Sergeant Flack came in. Frisnay said:

"Flack, take this down to the labs for an autopsy."

Flack picked up the cat by holding the four corners of the paper. "Poor pussy," he said.

"That thing died last night?"

"Ay."

"You might have let me have it a bit fresher." He looked round to make sure the window was wide open. Bishop said:

"It was too late to slip it under your pillow."

Frisnay drew hard on his cigarette and then said:

"You were saying?"

"Last night I was lurking nefariously in the grounds of the Kingston-Electric buildings. There was someone near me, waiting for me to move. I chucked a brick at the fence, and that cat bobbed up. It was shot at, instead of me. Later, I collected the corpse."

"There's a bullet in it?"

"No."

"How did you know it had died?"

"It fell down from the fence like a cold pudding. It impressed me."

Frisnay swung in his swivel-chair, easing his legs.

"Yes, it must have been impressive, a cat coming down disguised as a cold pudding."

"So I knew the man who was there must be Dr. Veiss."

Frisnay stopped swinging in the chair. After a little while he said:

"No noise?"

"The weapon is dead silent."

"No flash?"

"There was no noise, and no flash, when Jones fell dead in his cell at Pentonville."

Frisnay put the ends of his fingers together and counted them. Bishop added, "Derek Veiss was breaking into the technical station. That's why we were there—Vic Levinson and I. We took him away with us. I didn't think it was a good thing to leave him loafing about there, with his old man feeling so very hairspring in such bad light."

"You were lucky."

"Yes. But it'll help me, in future, to know that Veiss is so jumpy. If I find myself within a mile of him, again, I'm going to shout for Mum."

"You're a damned fool, sticking your neck out."

"It prevents a double-chin. Incidentally, the name of this charming little gas-lighter is the Z.69." He told Frisnay about the diary. Frisnay said:

"Veiss is holding the diary as a threat, to keep the boy straight?"

"It would seem logical."

"Certainly his record smells, for a kid of his years."

"Have you questioned them both?"

"Yes. There's no real alibi, in either case, for the night Thorburn was killed; but that's negative evidence." He paused, then said slowly, "You see, this is the problem for me, Hugo. It's got two angles. I'm trying to find out who killed Thorburn. If I do, it'll be when I find the weapon. The Special Branch is trying to find out more about the weapon: or the possibility of there being such a weapon. You're ahead of us there; you've even got a name for it. Now, if they get at it, actually see it for themselves, they hand me my murderer. So we're each working at one part of a two-part job."

"How can you lose?"

Frisnay put his hands flat on the desk.

"We can lose this way. If Veiss hadn't been so ready to use this weapon against Marilyn Thorburn, he could have yielded to pressure by the Special Branch and brought the Z.69 into the open without risking a murder charge—and certainly without risking his neck. Even with fresh evidence on the Jones death—that's to say the discovery of a weapon that *could have* killed him—we wouldn't be happy about making a charge; and no court would sentence him to death for killing a man due to die an hour later by execution, however much, technically, he would be a murderer. And evidence on the Madrid episode would be difficult, if not impossible to dig up. Following?"

"Try me: therefore, until Thorburn died, Veiss could have brought the Z.69 into the open. Now it's too late because he'd convict himself. In fact, unless you drop this case, and officially close the Thorburn murder, so that Veiss can never be put on trial, you and the Special Branch are working against each other, in effect."

"Quite. I know it. They know it. Veiss knows it. And no one can make a new move to break the deadlock."

"Unless," Bishop said casually, "the issue warrants a way round."

"What way?"

"Call it an arrangement, at high level. Collect all the evidence you can against Veiss and hand a case to the Public Prosecutor. Put Veiss on trial for the murder of Thorburn—"

"There's not enough evidence. He'd be acquitted."

"Precisely. He could then come into the open with the Z.69, without risk. He could hand over the murder-weapon for the benefit of his adopted country, knowing he can't be tried twice for the same crime."

Frisnay looked shocked. "We'd be rigging a murderer's pardon, under the nose of the public."

"And safeguarding the public against the risk of the Z.69 going off again—either at one person, anyone who gets in Veiss's way, or at a million people, in the name of war."

"War?"

"The Special Branch isn't worrying about someone else getting killed—just another one like Thorburn. It's worried about the whole country."

Frisnay shook his head. "I can't put it to anyone that we rig a case against Veiss, aiming deliberately at his certain acquittal. Any case I hand to the Prosecutor has to aim at his conviction."

Bishop got up.

He said, "Then it's a race for the Z.69. Competitors are you, the Special Branch, Craddock, Georgina Hutton, and me."

"What do you want the Z.69 for?"

"To turn it round the other way. At the moment it's pointing at me."

The telephone rang. Frisnay picked it up and said:

"Yes?" He listened, against the sound of the traffic. "All right. I'll go and see her myself." He hung up. He said, "Mrs. Veiss has been on the phone. Her husband is missing."

"So they've got him."

"Who?"

"Craddock's mob."

"Think so?"

"Ten to one."

Frisnay got up. "I must go and talk to Mrs. Veiss, and follow it up from there."

"Freddie."

"Well?"

"If Craddock's got Veiss, he's got the Z.69 as well."

Frisnay crossed to the door. "If you'll come down with me, you can leave a full description of this man Craddock. We'll get a priority signal out to docks and airports."

"And quick."

The room was quiet. Two of the lamps were burning, one on Bishop's desk, the other above the table where they were sitting with the checker-board. The Princess Chu Yi-Hsin, whose honorable ancestors had watched this game played in an ancient Royal House a world away, sat with her eyes half-closed, her tail half-curled, her small mind half-way between wakefulness and sleep.

Softly Miss Gorringe said, "I suggest you resign."

"M'm?"

"Your King's in exposed check, and you can

only put your Knight into hazard."

"I've given you a bad game."

"Well, patchy."

He moved the Red King.

"What's that all about?" she asked, surprised.

"I've resigned. And that one is Dr. Veiss."

He moved three other pieces. "Craddock. Georgina. Derek Veiss."

She moved a White Bishop. "You." A White Rook. "Freddie."

His hand toyed with the White Queen. He said, "Vic."

They looked at the pattern. She said in a moment:

"Poor old Veiss! Surrounded."

He knocked down the King. "If he's still alive."

"Ring the Yard again. Freddie might be there now."

He got up. After a delay, Frisnay came through on the line. He said:

"There's no news. I'm waiting, myself."

"Nothing on either of them?"

"Nothing. We're keeping a priority watch. So is the Special Branch."

"You're looking for them together, or singly?"

"Both. We want Craddock badly. Veiss is just missing from his home, officially. We're covering all contingencies but Veiss might merely have taken a sudden break from overwork and gone somewhere to get some peace; and Craddock might be at the pictures or a Turkish bath."

"He'll be steamed-up, wherever he is. I give you ten to one that—"

"I only bet on certainties. It *looks* as though Craddock has got hold of Veiss and the Z.69. We're working on that line. We shall find them both together, or we shall find only Craddock, if he's done away with Veiss and dropped the body in the Thames—"

"If you find Veiss, it won't be in the river. He'll be picked up somewhere—a sad victim of something people have been dying of for generations. Heart-failure. And we shall want Craddock under lock and key before anyone in this world can get another night's sleep—"

"All right, it's a crisis. Did you ring me to say that?"

That was definitely said with the edge off. Bishop said:

"Beg pardon, Inspector. I was just working over the situation in my mind, and—"

"Then go and ring your mind up, not me. When we get any news I'll tell you. Good night."

The line closed. Bishop put the receiver down. Miss Gorringe asked:

"Freddie given you anything?"

"Yes. A flea in my ear."

"He must be working like a black. This isn't the

kind of case where he can plod on to the bitter end—"

The telephone rang. Bishop picked it up and said:

"Yes?"

"Sorry, Hugo," Frisnay again. "I'm under pressure from all departments."

Bishop grinned gently. "That's all right, you mean-gutted rattlesnake."

Frisnay grunted eloquently and rang off again. Bishop looked obliquely at the pieces on the chessboard. They sat there in the lamplight, their shadows crowding. He dialled the number of the Red Queen.

She answered at once, but a little nervously. He said:

"My dear Georgina."

"Hugo? What's happened?"

He played for drama. "Guess."

There was a pause. "Veiss is there with you."

"No. But it's nice to know your reaction. You sound as if you're at the end of something. Would it be your tether?"

She said, "Can you come round here?"

"When?"

"Now."

"I don't think I'd better. The line of your evening gown might be ruined by bulges in wrong places—"

"No. This isn't a trap, Hugo. I give you my word."

Sweetly he said, "You'd break your word as cheerfully as my neck, if it suited you. But I'll come, at my own risk. Just give me five minutes to slip into something bulletproof."

He rang off. Miss Gorringe said:

"How big is the risk, Hugo?"

He gazed idly at the chessboard.

"One can never tell. They vary so."

"Craddock might be there."

"Yes. That's why I'm going. We want that man."

"You might be walking into a dead-end. I do mean dead."

"You've been reading Dan Dare."

She followed him into the hall. He put on his gloves. She said, "Take a gun."

"I'd be terrified of it. They make such a nasty bang." He opened the front-door. "If I'm not back by cock-crow, call out the Camel Corps."

She was on edge still. Her eyes were bright with nerves.

"Hugo—come in."

He looked round the tiny room. She turned away and said: "We'll have a drink."

He watched her. He said: "A completely unspoiled line."

"What?"

"Your house-coat."

She opened a bottle. "I told you it wasn't a trap."

He wandered about. "I like your little flat."

"Do you? Is gin all right?"

"And French?"

"Yes, there is some."

"This room has a definite atmosphere, redolent of enchanted midnights."

She brought him his gin. She was smiling, above zero.

"You're making me feel better already, Hugo. You're a remarkably quick-acting drug."

He took the drink, and sniffed it. She said, "Is there something wrong with it?"

"I don't expect so. But talking of quick-acting drugs, I just remembered I'm not necessarily among friends." He took a sip, and savored it. "But perfect."

"Please don't suspect me."

"I wouldn't dream of it." He was looking over her shoulder. It was still as difficult to do that as it had been at the party. He said, "And that's your bedroom, in there?"

Without heat she said, "Open for inspection."

He came back slowly, closing the bedroom door. "And that other door would be the kitchenette?"

She didn't answer. She stood near the window,

with her drink. He came back from the kitchenette. "All mod. con. I take it the bathroom is through the bedroom?"

She said, still not coldly, "You need a wash?"

"No. I just like to know the topography of a place. One has to have one's entrances... and one's exits. Particularly one's exits." His voice didn't change. "So you don't know where Craddock is."

"Should I?"

"You'd like to."

"Do you know?"

"No. With Veiss, probably."

She sounded edgy again. She was not on top of her form this evening. "Hugo, I—wish you could help me."

"But I can't."

"I know."

"Admittedly we're both working against Craddock, now that he's left you at the lych-gate; but that doesn't really put us in the same carriage. Try not to be upset." He was watching her, over his drink. She was nice to watch, in any case, apart from the fact that at any second she might pull a rapid trick.

She said, "You know my proposition. My orders are to get the Z.69, with or without any help. If Craddock leaves me, then I have to get it alone, single-handed."

"Surely that must appeal to your sense of the dramatic? A lone woman, gun on hip and nerves on edge, pitting her brains and beauty against—"

"Damn you, must you rub salt in?"

He thought her anger was more attractive than her cold bright calm. She drained her glass. "I know I'm losing points. I lost my gun, I lost you, I lost Craddock's help." She sank her voice. She was really going to mean this. "But if it's in me to do it, I'm getting the Z.69."

He raised an eyebrow. "You'd lose all, for that."

"All except my life."

"So there's a limit."

"I'm still young."

"Yes. And only the good die young. What made you imagine that Veiss was with me, when I rang?"

"Because he—" But she checked. "If you don't know, it wouldn't help me to tell you. As you say, we're not really working together. But Veiss isn't dead. The Z.69 is with him. And there's an itch, in his finger, for you."

She poured herself another drink. He said:

"But even if he'd called on me, I doubt if I would have been in any position to phone you, as I did. What makes you think he's still active?"

She stood facing him, with her glass filled. She said nothing. The smile was slightly pleased. There was something he didn't know. He said, "What makes you think that Craddock hasn't killed him by now?"

"He can't get near enough. Veiss has got his back to the wall. Craddock couldn't go close enough to kill him now. An army couldn't. We all want his new war-toy, and he wants to keep it. None of us can get near him; but he can get near us. When he does, we—"

His head moved as the telephone sounded. She looked worried as she picked up the receiver, as if all she wanted to do was to stop the bell ringing like that, getting on her nerves. She said:

"Yes?"

Bishop said quickly, "If it's Veiss, say I'm here."

She said into the phone, "Just a moment." She passed it to him. "For you."

He answered, and Vic said, "Hugo, it's me. Miss Gorringe told me you'd be at this number. Can you talk?"

"Not too much, no. But you can."

Georgina was standing by the window. He thought that from there she would just be able to catch a word now and then. He pressed the earpiece hard against his head.

Vic spoke quickly. "I've picked up Starling, the fat man. Our trails crossed. He's gone into a block of flats. I'm going to call on him, and see what I can find out."

"That's unwise."

"Perhaps, but he might know where Craddock is."

"He probably does, but he won't tell you."

"I must ring off, Hugo. It's becoming tricky—"

"Address?"

"Flat Nine, Wensford Close, South-west One."

"Might see you. Can't guarantee."

"I understand."

She rang off. He thought: last night we nearly got killed. If I don't go there now, I won't be able to think about anything else, or do anything else.

"You've lost your poise, darling."

She was smiling; it was a visible purr.

He nodded. "Yes. Any minute now and I topple right over." He took his hand off the telephone. "Would you forgive me if I went?"

"No."

"Then I must go, unforgiven."

The smile hardened. "Where are you going?"

"To see the maharajah about a jar of marmalade."

She was keeping anger down. "I'd rather you stayed. Could I persuade you?"

"Yes."

"How?"

"By knifing me in the spine. Have you a knife handy?"

"I wish to God I had."

"I thought you would."

She came to the door with him, her drink still in her hand. She said, "No ill feelings, Hugo."

"None in the world."

He went down to the car. It would take him ten or twelve minutes to reach S.W.1. He hoped she wouldn't do anything irrevocable, in that time. In twelve minutes Vic was liable to work through a twenty-four-hour shift. She was the impulsive type. He drove fast.

Wensford Close was behind a network of one-way streets that took him minutes to circulate, and when he saw the block of flats he saw too that there'd be no parking-space within a taxi-ride of here. He was cruising by, looking for a gap, when she came running across the pavement. He pulled up and she put her hands on the door-ledge and said:

"Someone's killed Starling."

13th MOVE

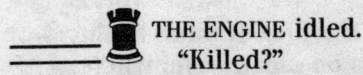

THE ENGINE idled.

"Killed?"

She was trying to steady herself. This had scared her.

"He was on the floor. I felt his heart." She moistened her dry lips. He said slowly:

"How long ago was it, Vic, when you followed him here?"

"I don't know. Twenty minutes, or thirty. I hung about, for a little, after I'd seen him go into—"

"Yes, I see." He was watching the street. It must have happened while she was phoning him. She had been a few minutes on the phone, first ringing Gorry, then having to ring Georgina's number. It had happened then. Fifteen minutes ago. "Look, you'd better climb in."

"Aren't you going to—?"

"Yes. In a minute."

She looked cold, pinched. He held the door open for her. A taxi came past, crawling through the gap. The sedanca was taking up half of what was left of the street, between the double ranks of parked cars.

"Vic, did you see anyone? Anyone else?"

She sat hugging her knees. "Only one man. He was going down the corridor, away from the flat where—Starling is."

"Was he hurrying?"

"No."

One man. In the corridor. It was a big block of flats. But there was one man, somewhere, with blood on his hands only fifteen minutes cold.

She said, "I'd—never seen one before." She was trying to apologize.

"They look a bit odd, don't they?"

His head turned slightly. A man was coming out of the flats, coming down the steps. "Vic, have you ever seen Dr. Veiss?"

"No. Why?"

"That's Dr. Veiss, turning along the pavement." He heard his own voice, sounding keyed up. That was the Red King, going along there. No one could get near him now. An army couldn't.

She was saying something but he touched her hand and said, "Can you drive this?" He didn't wait. She'd have to. He was getting out, shutting the door quietly.

"Hugo, I—"

"Listen. The engine's running. Gears are easy. Park it somewhere, or drive it to my place—"

"I want to come with you—"

"Sorry." His head went on turning slowly, keeping the walking man in sight. It was a long street. There was no immediate hurry. "I'll find you again, by phone."

"I'm coming with you."

"It's too—it's too complicated."

He walked away, passing between the bumpers of two parked cars, reaching the pavement below the flats. Then he stopped, and came back quickly. She was trying to find the gears.

"Vic, don't drive off yet. He mustn't see this car. And don't phone the police."

She didn't say anything, but just nodded. She was worried about the gears, about not going with him. He grinned faintly and said, "You look rather well, behind that wheel."

He hurried a little now, going down the pavement, seeing the narrow, diminishing figure ahead of him. He knew she wouldn't do anything that he had asked her not to. If she phoned the police, they'd be in this area by the platoon; and Veiss would panic when they closed in; and he had reached the stage, now, where he didn't know when to stop. This would have to be done quietly, and neatly, and quickly, before there was a chance of pulling that deadly thing out and using it.

Three Spaniards, and Jones. Thorburn next. Now Starling. Anyone, now, who got in his way.

The taxi slowed, its tires sizzling over the wet road. The one behind it pulled out, overtaking, then stopping, a short distance ahead. Bishop got out and gave some money to the driver. He was in the shop doorway when Veiss went across the pavement to the tube-station. Bishop counted five, and walked quickly past the tobacconist's window, turning to his left, entering the stairs down. He could still see Veiss. He was buying a ticket. This was the Edgware Line. Bishop took a ticket to the end, and stood at the top of the escalator. Veiss was not in sight now. He had come this way: to Platforms 1 to 4. He had been on this escalator. So he must have walked down its moving steps, to save time. Bishop walked down them too. If a train came in, and he couldn't find Veiss in time, it might make a lot of difference to everything.

The platforms were not crowded. He took the subway to 3 and 4, by nothing better than instinct. He shouldn't be this far behind in any case: if Veiss were on 1 or 2, and a train came in, he was going to take some finding again.

He wasn't on 3.

He was at the end of Platform 4, standing slightly away from a couple of foreign students. They were talking. Bishop heard the dry, bubbling sound of their accents as he walked slowly towards the end of 4. He had decided, in the last few seconds, to get Veiss now. Not trail him about and maybe risk exposure, involving other people in a crowded place, with Veiss ready to use that thing.

If he approached him direct, in the open, Veiss would hold his fire. If he tried to ham-string him in a dark street, or trip him in whatever place he was staying at, Veiss would fire. He had reached that condition of mind: the condition of the mind of a gambler who has been winning, and winning, and now is reckless, greedy, convinced of his unalterable luck. And also afraid, secretly, that all this could be lost in the next throw.

The students were talking quickly, their bright-sweatered bodies held forward to balance the weight of the rucksacks, their hands busy with folders, brochures, maps. Beyond them, Veiss stood looking down at the rails. For a moment Bishop thought he was contemplating the way out; down here it was so easy; but there was nothing dejected in the set of his shoulders. Slight though they were, there was a suggestion of power in their deliberate hunch. Like Atlas, little Veiss carried the world.

Footsteps sounded hollow, down the hard, echoing platform.

Quietly, "Good evening, Dr. Veiss."

Bland face, glint of gold spectacles framing eyes that looked strained. A moment, to register the fact that Bishop was here. A moment, to pre-control the voice.

"Mr. Bishop. I have been hoping to meet you."

"I know."

The right hand buried in the right pocket of the coat; the body held to face Bishop's.

"I did not think," Veiss said, "it would be in a place like this."

"It's rather public, for your purposes."

"My purposes. Yes. Major Craddock told me about you—"

"Craddock was lying—"

"You are bound to say that. I cannot believe you both, and there is no time, now, to consider." The tone grew plaintive. "I am being driven so hard, Mr. Bishop." He shook his head slightly. "So many people are trying—"

"We'll go somewhere more private," Bishop said. They kept their voices low. Two men, acquaintances, waiting for their train, filling in the moment with conversation. "Somewhere," Bishop said, "where we can talk."

"No."

Bishop said, "Then, some other time." He would follow Veiss, all through the night, if he had to.

"I cannot risk more danger, to my wife, my family, or myself." The tone now reflective, then petulant: "If only you had all left me alone..."

Bishop said, "Are you carrying the Z.69 with you now?"

The spectacles swung up, focusing.

"How do you know its name?"

"I know more than its name. I know what it can do, and I know what it has done. I could help you, if you cared to let me. You want help, badly."

"Nothing can harm me now." His hand, inside the pocket, seemed to move. "Nothing."

"People who get in your way," said Bishop, "are—"

"They should not get in my way! They are senseless. Like you—you are stupid, coming here to meet me when you know I must get you out of my way—"

"I'll strike a bargain with you, Veiss—"

"You are in no position. Don't you see that?"

The silence, the expectant silence down here where the train was overdue, where all trains were always overdue and home was a mirage, became slowly charged with a murmur that came creeping from the tunnel-mouth. The air vibrated with it, minutely.

"If you kill me out of hand, you'll hang."

People shifted their feet, turned to face the tunnel-mouth, hitched their parcels more securely in their hands.

Veiss had not moved. His body was turned towards the rail-channel at fifteen or twenty degrees, almost facing it. Facing him was Bishop, his back to the channel. Under their feet, the stone vibrated; around them, the air trembled. The sound slowly took on identity, rising to a train's moan.

"No one will ever know. No one can ever hang me."

The voice was uneasy and thin. The eyes began flickering as if the rising sound were a rising light, beginning to dazzle him.

"Veiss, there's a train coming."

"Yes."

"We'll get into it, and find a place to talk—"

"It is too late to talk."

The moan loudened. Air came past, brushing their faces with its stale warmth. The two students raised their voices, pitching them above the sound.

"You won't stand a chance, if you kill me. They know Starling's dead. They know I followed you—"

"They can do nothing. I am safe."

ROOK'S GAMBIT

His slight body was rigid. The flicker touched his eyes and he narrowed them. Their rims reddened, slowly, as the warm dust raced by. His voice whistled in the dark. "I shall always be safe."

This is what he looks like, then, when he kills. This is what he looked like with Thorburn, and Starling. Screwing himself up to do it. Not the cold, unimaginative triumph of a killer whose ego demands the death; but the nervy desperation of someone who must do something he hates doing, has hated doing before.

"Veiss."

Their voices were sibilant, straining above the rush of sound as the train exploded from the tunnel-mouth, slowing.

"Step back." The stiff little body turned a degree and the hand moved again, in the pocket. "Step back!"

"Veiss, don't be a fool. You'll die too."

"Back!"

The face changed, in this final second, as he drove himself. The face wore all the evil that must be in a man to kill at all, however much good there is besides.

"Step back!"

Bishop knew, now, that reason was still in the man's mind. He didn't want this to be another victim of "heart-failure." He wanted it to be an accident. If Bishop would not die by accident, under the train, then he must use the Z.69. Because, by some means, he must die. But better by accident.

The air steadied as the train slowed, its moan dying by infinite degrees. It would be almost behind him now. In a second, two seconds at most, there would be no chance of an accident. Veiss would fire. No sound. No flash. Just a man falling.

Two seconds. One.

As he fell into the channel, he spun his body round to face it. His brain registered photographic scenes: Veiss, standing there. Then the curve of the tunnel. The motorman's cab, sliding towards him. Then the rails, bridging their fat white insulators.

One of the students screamed.

14th MOVE

A MAN'S voice rose against the scream of the girl. The train jarred to a halt. The air-compressor pulsed, an inane whinny.

"Shift it back!"

Men were running. The girl was sobbing, shocked. The motor-man's face was white in the window of his cab. He set the train running back, inching it. A porter was keeping people away from its side, his voice strained.

"Back—back more." The train crawled.

Someone said, "There he is."

A man came running back from the offices at the end of the platform. "Switched off!"

"Eh?"

"We're switched off!"

A man jumped down, landing between the rails. Someone said, "He's moving!"

The man was bent over Bishop. Bishop dug his

hand into the dirt again, trying to lever himself up.

"You're okay, mate—you'll be okay."

"Help me up."

"Ye'—you'll be okay, mate. You jus'—"

"Hurry."

Bishop came up like a windmill, trying too hard to get his brain going, his body working.

"Easy, mate. Jus' take it—"

"Phone. Telephone. Help me to get—"

"Take it easy, for—"

"Telephone." He pushed the man away and made a lunge at the edge of the platform where a knot of people was gathered. Hands reached down. He skinned a shin and lost one of his shoes as they took his hands, dragging him up. He thought: this is how the angels catch a man up from hell.

"Telephone—"

"You're all right. You've had a bad shock—"

"Keep clear, there—let him breathe—"

He pushed at them, half-tripping. Someone saved him. He ran his eyes along the platform wall and saw the two narrow doorways. He stumbled towards them, throwing off someone's hands. The man who had jumped down into the channel was dodging after him— "Take it easy. You're in no fit state—"

"Where's your telephone?"

"Now listen—"

"Damn you, where's the phone?"

He went pitching into the first doorway. Two telephones were on the lift-up desk. He tugged a receiver up as if it weighed a ton, and stood leaning against the wall, his other hand dialling.

"Look 'ere, you can't—"

"Leave me alone."

Two, three white faces, peering at him, not understanding. Prepared to be officious in their relief.

"I'll 'ave to 'ave your name and address, please—"

Into the phone Bishop said, "Police."

A man came into the office and tried to take the receiver away but Bishop caught him smartly with his elbow.

"Operations, listen, Dr. Veiss—" He had to draw a breath and let it out sharply, to stop the dizziness. "Dr. Veiss has just left Morden Way tube-station on foot, or in taxi. You got that?"

"Morden Way tube-station—"

"Listen. He's carrying the Z.69."

"Carrying what, sir?"

"Tell Mr. Frisnay. Carrying the Z.69. That's important."

"Z—69. Can I have your name, please?"

The office swayed. He righted it.

"Bishop. Go like hell."

"Oh, it's you, Mr. Bishop. Yes, we'll go like hell."

He dropped the receiver. The place dipped away again, but he got it back straight. There was too much to do before he could fall over.

The sergeant said into the mouthpiece, "And get hold of the Super. Tell him it's urgent. Tip off the Special Branch. You got that?" He glanced across the room. To the man by the panels he called, "All right, Jim."

The man snapped down the switches.

"Action all cars area T to Z. All cars area T to Z—action. Dr. Veiss—Dr. Veiss left Morden Way—Morden Way tube-station one minute ago."

KB-3, stationary in Haligrove Road, facing north, started up. The hollow, metallic voice held volume above the engine's sound.

"One minute ago. He is armed. Special precautions must be taken."

The rear tires clipped a cigarette packet from the gutter, slewing against the ribbed metal drain-grill as the car turned east.

"If he threatens, hold off. He is prepared to kill. He is prepared to kill."

KB-6 gypped the lights at amber and was whipped into third, with full throttle taking it past the lorry just below sliding-point on the wet road.

"Keep him in sight, once located. Do not lose him."

Two cyclists were abreast, passing a bus. KB-6 gave them the bell, slicing inch-close to a street-bollard and catching the lights at green, south towards Morden Way.

"If possible, get him away from crowded places. Do not lose him, once located."

KB-1 crossed Picadilly at Dover Street, gonging a gap between two cabs and an *Evening News* van.

"This is action all cars area T to Z. Send in locations. Locations, please. KB out."

"Hello, KB. Going south towards Morden Way along Edgware Road—KB-6 over."

"Hello, KB. Turning east into Marylebone Road towards Morden Way—KB-3 over."

"Hello, KB. Joining KB-9 at junction Morden Street and High Road, heading towards Morden Way station. KB-1 over."

The Super came in.
"Sarn't Cox, are you on top line?"
"Yes, sir, we're on top line."
"If we can, we get Veiss tonight."
"Yes, sir. Tonight."

Vic and Miss Gorringe were standing by the smaller window, that overlooked the end of the mews, when Bishop came into the room. Vic took a step towards him. Miss Gorringe looked at him, over the girl's shoulder. Vic said pointlessly:
"Hugo?"
Miss Gorringe sighed. She said:
"I hesitate to pry, but have you just been passed through a concrete-mixer?"
He touched the girl's hand, then turned away from her, dropping into a chair.
"No, I missed a train, just."
"Anything dislocated?"
"Only the engine-driver's front teeth. He stopped in a hurry. Has Freddie phoned?"

"No." She crossed the room, to the alcove. "If you're not bleeding, you'd better have a brandy."

"Make it a glass of water, Gorry. I've got a mouthful of tickets to Tooting." He got up restlessly. "Why hasn't Freddie phoned? It's nearly eleven." He picked up the phone and dialled. Miss Gorringe asked the girl:

"What for you, my dear?"

"A quick gin, please."

"Quick?"

"I think it'll have to be. We're in the middle of a high-pressure belt just now."

Bishop put the phone down. Gorry said:

"Out?"

"Yes."

She held his glass of water. She said, "Will you drink it, or shall I throw it over you?"

"Don't nag me; I'll wash in a minute."

"Can we know what happened?"

He swallowed half the water and said irritably, "I flung myself under a tube-train."

Miss Gorringe set her face and said, "Wasn't that rather impulsive?" Then she turned back to the alcove and poured herself a drink. A double. Vic said:

"Did Veiss have the Z.69 with him?"

His mind swung, looking for the answer. That's right, she was there in the car when young Veiss had told him about the Z.69.

"Yes," he said. He finished the water. Blood was caking his sock, from the grazed shin. He was beginning to feel third-rate all over. "He wanted this one to look like an accident, heart-failure being so suspect these days. If I'd stayed my ground, he would have had no option but to fire. So I chose the channel between the live rails and emulated a flat-fish."

Miss Gorringe watched him. "You were lucky not to come out filleted. I don't know how long my nerves are going to stand working for you. If any—" She broke off on a faint yelp as the telephone shrilled. Bishop was there in a few strides, picking it up.

"Yes?"

"Veiss has slipped us, Hugo."

Frisnay's voice was rough. Bishop checked his thoughtless comment. He said, "A pity."

Frisnay grunted. "We threw a cordon two miles deep."

"Never mind. You'll get him."

"Yes, we'll get him." He added, "I've had a report about a man falling under a tube-train at Morden Way. Was that you?"

"Yes?"

"For Pete's sake. Are you all right?"

"Skinned a fetlock, that's all. I'm sorry we've lost him. It was a near cop."

"You did your best. So did we. The men are still out there, combing. I suppose you're in bed, are you?"

"No. Are you?"

"Course not, you fool. I haven't been under a train."

"You going home, Freddie?"

"No. Not for a long time."

He sounded too angry to sleep. Bishop said:

"Spare me half an hour. Something I want to show you."

"Another dead cat?"

"Dead bird, this time."

"What?"

"Name is Starling. Come round and we'll go and have a look at him—"

"Do I understand there is a dead man you want to show me?"

"That's it, Freddie. I was going to ring you before, but then I felt so very run-down in the tube-station, and—"

"His name is what?"

"Starling."

"Where is he?"

"Flat Nine, Wensford Close, South-west One."

There was a pause while Frisnay wrote it down. "I'll send a patrol-car there, ahead of us."

"You're on your way?"

"Yes."

Bishop came away from the telephone, and poured himself some more water. He said, "They lost Veiss. Never mind."

"Freddie's coming here to pick you up, Hugo?"

He nodded. Vic said, "Shouldn't you go to bed?"

"Eventually. So should we all." He moved to the door. "I'll get a cold shower before Freddie comes. Vic, what d'you want to do?"

"Stick."

She looked prettier when she was worried. Her eyes were wider. He said:

"Look after each other. If any stranger calls, shoot him in the stomach and then ask him for his card." He went out of the room.

The atmosphere was different in here now, because he was back, alive. They hadn't been very confident about that, while they were waiting for news.

Vic said in a moment, toying with her zippered note-book:

"You have an exciting life, Miss Gorringe. I envy you."

"My dear, your own seems far from dull."

"But I haven't—" She closed the zipper with a jerk. "I mean you work with Hugo. That must be something quite unique."

Miss Gorringe looked sad, about something. She said:

"Unique would be a word, perhaps." She waited for a moment before she said, "I take it that in the last few days he's fired your imagination."

Vic said, "I lost my cigarettes somewhere. I—"

"I'm sorry—there, in the box."

"One for you?"

"Please."

They used the table-lighter. It seemed minutes before the silence was broken.

Miss Gorringe said, "Yes, that does happen."

"Regularly." The word, with barely the intonation of a question, dropped out unhappily.

"Vic, you know who I am. Hugo's factotum extraordinary without portfolio. His friend too. I love most of his friends, and nearly get killed by most of his enemies. People, in his odd life, come and go. Some stay. Not many. They become his friends, our friends. Among the others are those who'd like to possess him exclusively. They never will. Nobody ever could."

Feebly: "He's self-possessed."

"Apart from other things."

"I'd like another drink, please. Sober me up."

Miss Gorringe spoke softly. "No, don't sober up. Hang on to the dream. If it never comes true, at least you'll have had a wonderful fling—"

"There must have been so many of us, at

different times, sitting here and talking about him because we had to talk about him to someone, preferably someone who knows him well." The tone was over-bright, too careless. "Mustn't there?"

Miss Gorringe had reached the sideboard.

"It was gin, wasn't it?"

The girl's voice sounded crisply amused.

"Yes, it was gin."

She was sandwiched between Bishop and Frisnay, in the back of the car. The car nosed through light traffic toward S.W.1. Frisnay said:

"Did you see the body yourself?"

Bishop said, "No. I went after Veiss instead."

"Miss Levinson, did you see Dr. Veiss in the building anywhere?"

She eased her left arm free. Bishop shifted, giving her more room. "Yes, but I didn't know who it was at that time. He was going down one of the corridors—"

"Hurrying?"

"No, walking quite normally." She looked through the side-windows. "It's just round the corner from here—"

"It's all right, our driver knows. Did you see anyone else in the corridors?"

"A woman, middle-aged, with two others,

ROOK'S GAMBIT

younger. No one else, I think."

"You'll give me a full statement later, of course."

"Yes. How much can I use, in my paper?"

"Not a word, yet." The car turned, and began slowing to a crawl through the narrow avenue of parked vehicles. "The Press is co-operating with us, all along the line, until we can break the full story. When that happens, at least you'll have been in closer touch with events than anyone else. For you it'll be a scoop. Hang on to that sweet thought."

He opened the door when the car stopped. He and Bishop got out. She said, "Can I come up with you?"

He said, "You found the body. It gives you the privilege."

On the first floor they met one of the patrols. He was from the car Frisnay had sent ahead.

"Well?"

"There's no answer from Flat Nine, sir."

"It doesn't surprise me. The tenant is dead. Didn't you go in?"

"The door's locked, sir."

Bishop glanced once at Vic. Frisnay said: "Locked?"

She said, "When I left, it was ajar."

"So you told me. Brown, give another ring, in case we're mistaking the number."

"Yes, sir."

"But this was the number," she said. "The door was ajar."

Frisnay said nothing. Brown pressed the bell again, and leaned his head against the door-panel, listening. In half a minute Frisnay said, "It's a ten-story building, and all the passages will look alike—"

"It was Nine," she said, biting it out cleanly.

Bishop said, "The light's not too bright along here—"

Then the door opened and a man stood there, in his pyjamas. He had a lop-sided face with careful eyes and good jaw-line.

"Look here, this is the tenth time that bell's rung, and I'm trying to get some sleep. Now what is it?"

Frisnay said in a moment, after a swift up-and-down glance, "I'm sorry to disturb you, sir. We're making enquiries, and we seem to have mistaken the number. We're anxious to see a man called Starling."

"Well, my name's Petman." He ruffled his hair, cutting off a yawn. "So that's not much help to either of us. Now if I go back to bed, you won't ring the bell again, will you?"

Frisnay smiled. He smiled whenever he was undecided. The last time Bishop had seen him smile was two years ago at a circus. "You don't

ROOK'S GAMBIT

know which flat Mr. Starling has, do you sir?"

"Surely I'd have told you when you said who you were looking for?" The careful eyes looked out of the lop-sided face at Frisnay. Frisnay said:

"Yes, quite. Would you mind if I took a quick look inside here, sir?"

Petman blinked. "Of course I'd mind. How can I get my sleep with a lot of people poking about in my flat?"

"No, sir. Just two of us, for a quick glance round."

"You'll need a warrant, you know."

Frisnay had stopped smiling. "I'll have to fetch one, then. That'll mean knocking you up again later. I'd hate to do that, Mr. Petman."

Petman grunted impatiently, "Oh all right, all right. You can come in, but don't go knocking things over. I've got a lot of valuable pieces in here, and it's not fully insured."

He turned, going back into the room. Frisnay murmured:

"Miss Levinson, come inside with me, will you?"

She nodded. Petman was standing in the middle of the lounge, re-tying his pyjama-cord.

"Now what d'you want to do? Turn the place upside—"

"Just a moment, sir." Quietly to the girl, "Is this the flat?"

Her eyes were wide, "No. It isn't."

"Make quite certain."

"It's—not the same flat."

Frisnay looked up at Petman.

"Thank you, sir. We shan't worry you again."

"I should hope not."

Frisnay and Vic came back to the softly-lighted passage. Petman shut the door, with a little more force than was necessary. Frisnay said to the patrol-man, "Brown. Start at the top of this block and check every door. Don't ring any bells. If you see anyone still about, ask them if they know which flat Mr. Starling has. It'll be one of the flats directly above this one, or maybe the one below, on the ground floor."

"Yes, sir." He went loping steadily along the passage towards the lift. Vic said between firm teeth:

"It was this flat. Nine."

Frisnay didn't look at her. "But when we were inside you told me—"

"I know. I don't understand it, any of it. But it was Flat Nine. Nothing will shake me on that."

Bishop said, "And there was a dead man inside?"

She dug her small hands into her trench-coat. "There was a dead man, and it was Starling. I saw his face. I'd followed him here myself."

"You followed him," Frisnay said, "to this door?"

"Yes." Her face looked strained. "Then I went to phone Mr. Bishop, so that someone should know where I was going, in case there was—any trouble. I wasn't away more than six or seven minutes."

"And when you got back?"

"This door was ajar. I pushed it wider, and looked in. Starling was on the floor. I bent over him and—and touched him. He was dead."

"Cold?"

"I only felt his chest." Her hands were tight, in the pockets of her trench-coat. "No, he wasn't cold."

"And that is exactly as it happened?"

"Exactly."

Frisnay began walking towards the entrance-hall. "Except that it wasn't Flat Nine."

She followed him, with Bishop. She said:

"Don't think me stupid, Mr. Frisnay, but—"

"Freddie," Bishop said. "We should try Flats Three, Six and Eight. They all look rather like Nine in this light—"

She said with small, quick defiance, "But it was *that* door. The second from the end of the passage."

"Yes," Frisnay said. He went on walking.

"Don't you think I'd admit to making a mistake? A reasonable one? I was coming out of a dead man's flat, and I'd never seen one before, a dead man. And the light's not good. I could easily have made a mistake."

"Yes," Frisnay said. They neared the entrance-hall.

"Quite simply," she said, "I haven't. That was the door, and that was the number."

A voice asked, "Some trouble, is there?"

Frisnay turned. "Who are you?"

A shambling, seedy man with a cigarette-end gone out but still in his mouth. "Me? Caretaker. Who are you?"

"Detective-inspector Frisnay, New Scotland Yard."

"Oh, lumme." The cigarette-end wobbled.

"You'll know which flat Mr. Starling has, I imagine?"

"Who?"

"Star-ling."

"Star-lin'? No. Don't know anyone o' that name, sir." He put his head on one side like a sparrow in a dust-bath. "There's Martin—Parker—Chalmers—them are as near as I can get."

"Who lives in Flat Nine?"

"Flat Nine ... Flat Nine ... " The pert head came upright. "That's Mr. Petman."

"How long has he been there?"

"Mr. Petman? Two or three munce, it'd be. Come 'ere in Febr'y. Some trouble, is there?"

"Would it surprise you?"

ROOK'S GAMBIT

"Eh? Trouble? Ye'. We don't often get trouble 'ere."

Frisnay turned away. "You're lucky. You should be in my job."

Brown came down the stairs as they reached the entrance hall.

"Well?"

"Nothing unusual, sir. No doors ajar, no excitement."

"All right, get back to your car and keep watch on this building until you get a signal."

"Yes, sir." He went out through the main doors. The stillness in the entrance hall was stone-like. There was stone under their feet; the walls were stone. They were standing in a high dusty tomb. Her voice came clearly.

"You're furious with me, aren't you, Mr. Frisnay?"

"No. We can all make mistakes, Miss Levinson."

"I'm not, this time. It was Flat Nine, the second door from the end of that passage."

He went out to the steps with them. He said:

"Of course it was, and the only trifling difference is that instead of a dead man called Starling inside, there's a live one called Petman."

They got into the car and he sat forward to make room for her. "Miss Levinson, I'd appreciate a fully detailed statement from you, as soon as we reach my office. You must understand that all I'm interested in is finding the murderer of Marilyn Thorburn. If there was in fact a dead man in this building, it may or may not help me in my enquiries, and unless it ties up with my present case, someone else will automatically have the task of dealing with it."

The car started off, passing the other black saloon that was tucked in to the kerb with the lights off. "If you want to retract anything you've said, do that in your statement, because it'll help, and not hinder, and, as I've already pointed out, you could easily have made an understandable mistake. You agreed with me on that. Just get the facts quite right in your mind, and we'll fit them together in our own way. That clear?"

"Quite clear."

She was sitting in one of the small upright chairs, her zippered note-book tucked against her arm. Bishop was walking moodily from the filing-cabinets to the desk, and back. After a long time she said:

"He doesn't believe me. Do you?"

He stopped and looked down at her.

"Yes. I'm just trying to think of the answer."

"But you believe me, Hugo?"

He nodded. "Yes."

The door opened and Frisnay said:

"Sorry to have kept you." He sat down behind his desk. "I've just been to see the Assistant Commissioner."

Bishop said, to make Vic feel less miserable, "Inspector Frisnay flies high."

Frisnay grunted. "He also flies late. It's gone midnight and I'm still at my desk. I shall grow plants in here tomorrow. I like a bit of a garden where I live."

Bishop was pleased. Frisnay, too, was trying to make her feel less miserable. There must be some reason for that, because Frisnay was on a murder-job, and a small-time reporter's feelings mattered less than the dust. Either he had thought over her statement, and was beginning to believe in it, or fresh evidence had come to hand, supporting it. Bishop decided not to ask.

"Miss Levinson, I've got to talk to Mr. Bishop for a moment on a top-secret matter. I should ask you to go, now that you've given us your statement; but if you want to, you can stay. It might help us. I must warn you, though, that you're in on a very tricky official secret that might not mean much to a member of the public; but it could cost me my job if you didn't keep it strictly to yourself. If you stay, it'll be on those terms. If you want to go, it's your choice."

His face was wooden. He looked at her for a

moment, and asked, "What will you do?"

"Stick."

"So be it. Now I've taken your statement to the Assistant Commissioner. You didn't alter a word of it from your first story, and that gives me confidence in you, despite what we didn't find at the flats to support it. You may know that there's more involved in this enquiry than the death of Marylin Thorburn. You may imagine that *if* this man Starling died tonight in the block of flats from which Mr. Bishop followed Veiss, it might help us to get Veiss more quickly and more surely. So if your facts are right, it gives us a big chance. You'll have done a great deal for us."

He swung his head. "Hugo, you can do more."

Bishop was beginning to feel less third-rate. Some kind of dipsy-doodle was about to work. Even the A.C. was on the job. He murmured:

"Delighted."

"This man Petman," Frisnay said. "He behaved as an innocent man aroused from bed. He never made a slip—and by God I was looking for one. The only support that Miss Levinson has for her statement is that I've been a policeman for twenty-two years and I can recognize the criminal type through a brick wall in a thick fog."

He paused. Bishop said:

"You think Petman's a wrong 'un."

"Yes."

"So do I. And you're in a spot."

"I am. I've got a search-warrant—Flat Nine, Wensford Close. I could go there now with a regiment and turn the place skin-side in. But we don't want to show our hand either to Petman or Veiss, or anyone else who might be working with them."

"You want to check up on the flat, the quiet way."

Frisnay nodded. "We can't use a skeleton key, because if Petman found us there, and didn't happen to be involved in anything criminal, we'd stand an all-time rap."

Bishop mooched cheerfully across to the window.

"You'd better," he said, "hire an ex-con, who's a bit of a kitten with the keys."

"We're hiring you."

Bishop turned round.

"Well, well. What do they get, these days, for breaking and entering?"

"You'd get a big hand from the Assistant Commissioner."

"I'm dazzled. I shall write a series for the *Daily Burp*. 'I was a Stooge for Scotland Yard.'"

Frisnay said, "Are you going to do it?"

"I was going to do it anyway, old ducks."

Frisnay's face splintered.

"Then why the hell didn't you say so?"

"Because now I've got your official blessing I shan't spend the next six months on Dartmoor grinding granite into talcum-powder for prison-warders' wives."

"Hugo, this isn't any official blessing." He let that sink in. "This is an extreme measure, very small in itself, involving protection of the public on a grand scale. Otherwise we couldn't so much as drop you a hint on the subject. We're all sitting on dynamite, and for the moment you're holding the fuse."

Bishop said, "Charming. Has anyone got a light?"

Vic said, "Hugo."

"M'm?"

"Can I come with you?"

"As far as the block of flats. After that, Flannelfoot creeps alone."

He left her to look after his car. Just as a routine matter, the car was parked in the mouth of a yard, pointing into the roadway, ready to go.

He went up to the first floor and spent ten minutes at the lock of Flat Nine. He got the door open with as much racket as a beetle makes beating the air. Then he spent ten minutes inside the flat, with a pin-ray torch. Then he stepped back and knocked into a desk. Something on the desk rocked for a moment, but didn't fall. It was a piece of Bristol; he knew that, because in his mind, now, he held a complete inventory of the flat. He thought it was time he went, because it had been a lot of noise.

He reached the door, and Petman said:

"Don't move, will you?"

Bishop sighed briefly. "No."

The ceiling-light was snapped on. The room swam, glaring.

In a moment, "You're Bishop. You were here with the police."

Bishop was able, now, to see him clearly, as his eyes accommodated in the glare. Petman was still in his pyjamas, but his eyes were fresh. He hadn't been asleep.

"Yes," Bishop said. "And now I'm here without them."

"What are you looking for?" The gun moved a little, confidently drawing a bead.

"Starling's body."

"Can't find it?"

"Can't seem to find it anywhere. Shame, isn't it?"

Petman looked at him with his careful eyes and said:

"Set a thief to catch a thief. Maybe it takes a dead man to find a corpse." His face was beginning to sweat with the sour excitement that comes into them when they realize what they are going to do. "What's the shortest prayer you know, Bishop? Because you're on your way out of this world."

15th MOVE

"PETMAN THINK twice."

He didn't like the sweat on Petman's face. He liked it when they looked more cocky, less sick. You could work on them then, and twist their vanity round until it took their guard down. Then you could go in, and often get away with it.

But this one was sick about what he was going to do. It was a fetish with him, like tearing the wings off flies, or looking through keyholes in the bathroom doors, or blowing up toads with straws. This was the type that killed dirty. The more you talked about what they were going to do, the more they fed on its fascination, until they just squeezed the thing, as easy as falling in love with a slut. Death was a slut, this way.

"They've told me about you, Bishop." The face was tilted to the left, making up for its lopsidedness, so that it looked almost straight. "You're tricky, they say. All right be tricky now."

Bishop began moving his right foot, but had to stop as Petman said with a spitting thinness, "No, don't move . . . don't move. That isn't tricky; it's corny."

Bishop waited. There was nothing he could do yet. There might be nothing he could do ever. The risks varied. He looked down the muzzle of the gun and listened to the voice. It was something to do while he was waiting.

"I'll get quite a kick out of this. Petman? Who the hell's Petman?—Don't you know? The one who rubbed out Bishop."

Impatiently Bishop said, "Then start rubbing—or are you scared of that thing?"

The careful eyes were bright.

"Nothing scares me. Nothing."

"You lack imagination, then. A lot of things scare me." He sized Petman up and tried out the horror technique. "Think of the rope, for instance. It's made of new hemp. They always give you a new one. You can smell it when they drop it round your neck—you can smell the hemp, and for the first time in your life you realize that hemp is the worst smell on earth. And in—"

"Shuddup." It came quietly.

"And in the rope there's a metal eyelet, so that

when you drop with your legs kicking and your scream cut off—"

"Shuddup, will you?"

Louder that time. For some reason, he was listening. Perhaps he was picturing it, just as Bishop was telling him. Perhaps he was fascinated by this fetish too. The smell of hemp.

"I was talking to Hurst," said Bishop, "once, when he was off-duty. He's a mild little man; you'd never dream he had a job like that. And he told me he'd never had a man come to him on his feet. Either they crumple at the knees when they get near the trap, or they start struggling, and have to be—"

"That's enough." The gun-hand moved. When the slug didn't come tearing into his vitals, Bishop felt surprised. Petman was the hair-spring type.

"Sorry. But you're still a young man. What are you—forty? Forty-five? So much to miss—the sunshine, the drinks, the women—"

"I don't go in for women—"

"I'll bet they go in for you. Shame to spoil it all. You know, when your feet start kicking the air, the face turns blue, and the tongue sticks out like a stiff—"

"You don't scare me."

That was quite right. He'd nearly been scared; the sweat had gathered fast; then he'd taken a grip, as a man fights down sickness.

The technique was no good. It hadn't worked.

"You don't scare me, Bishop. You're as good as dead. I'm talking to a dead man."

"You don't know their language, but you will."

"Why did you come here? Why can't you keep out of—"

"Don't talk, Petman. Shoot. Nothing scares you. Shoot."

"You know why I don't—yet? I like this. I'm enjoying it."

"You're not. You're sweating like a pig—"

"Excitement. I'm excited, having you here without a hope in hell. Bishop, trussed up for grilling . . . think what they'll say."

Bishop stopped trying to edge nearer the desk. At the speed he was making, he wouldn't be near enough until next week—near enough to do anything. He said:

"Yes, think what they'll say. 'And you will be taken to a place of execution . . . and hanged by the neck until you are dead.'"

"I don't scare."

"You do. You all do. When a man has to carry a gun, it's because his nerve's gone, or because he never had one. When I meet a man with a gun, I know I'm on top, because he'll crack like a doll—"

Petman sucked in his breath as the telephone

rang and said, "Don't move—don't move—"

"I wasn't going to." The bell drilled through their heads. Petman picked up the receiver. He didn't take his eyes away from Bishop once. He watched all the time. He said:

"Who is it?"

Bishop could hear a woman's voice. It sounded like Georgina's. Petman said, "How do you know?" The plastic of the receiver was misting to the heat of his hand. He said, "No, don't come up. You're out now. The Major told me." There was no change in his eyes, but he must have been thinking hard. "Where are you?"

She said something, and then the line clicked dead.

He dropped the receiver. Bishop said:

"So you don't go in for women."

"Not for that one. She's prussic acid."

"But she's on her way."

"This is business."

"You don't sound so scared now, Petman. You're not having to screw your guts up to shoot. You've got a reprieve—"

"*Shuddup.* Think I've never shot a man? They do down cold; it's easy."

"Wipe the sweat off your face. It's unhygienic."

The doorbell rang. It startled Bishop. Georgina

must have phoned from the entrance-hall. Petman said:

"Don't move. Face this way." He backed carefully towards the door, watching Bishop hard. Bishop watched him steadily. It was a comical scene, a man walking backwards, another standing and watching him. It was about as comical as a snake boxed-in with a mongoose.

Petman touched the door, and moved his free left hand, feeling for the knob. He turned it, and pulled the door open an inch, and said over his shoulder:

"Come inside, but don't spoil my aim."

Vic came in, and Bishop said, "Behind the knees," and she brought one foot up in a beautiful swing, doubling Petman's knees so that his head jerked back. Bishop slipped on the carpet as he lunged forward, but it didn't wreck his chances. Petman's head was just coming forward nicely; then it went back again with a snap; there were knuckleprints on the jaw. Vic caught the gun and gave it to Bishop. Petman crashed into the door as he went down. He wasn't out. He sat there like a sack, doubled up, looking at them. A string of saliva came down from his mouth, tinted with blood.

"Who's this kid?"

Bishop was surprised that he was interested. It couldn't matter much who the kid was. He said:

"Forgive me. Mr. Petman—Miss Levinson." He pressed his knuckles into his handkerchief.

"But it was Hutton on the phone."

Vic said. "No. That was me."

"Where the hell did you come from?" He looked really mean now.

"I came with Mr. Bishop. I was listening outside the door—a smutty little trick I picked up at my prep-school. I heard you say something about rubbing out. I'm rather fond of Mr. Bishop, so I thought I'd just phone. Wouldn't you be more comfy with a cushion? You look so awkward, all elbows and eyeballs—"

"You stupid little bitch, I'll—"

"Oh, come now, Mr. Petman," Bishop murmured. "Let's remember our manners, or I'll throttle you on the installment system." He stopped murmuring. "Get up."

"I'll see you—"

"Get up, Petman."

He slid his shoulders up the wall, supporting himself with one hand on the bureau. Bishop thought he was coming for him, so he slipped the gun into his pocket and hung his hands ready. He said:

"What happened to Starling's body?"

"I don't know anything about—"

"Come on, Petman—"

"I tell you I don't—"

"You'd better try—"
"You can ask me till—"
"I'm going to. Where is Starling's body? Quick."
"I don't know what you're—"
"Vic."
"Yes?"
"Would you go outside for a minute? I know you can't bear the sight of blood."
"Yes, all right."
She turned toward the door.
Petman said thickly, "They took it away."
"You're too late. I want the whole story, and that'll take persuasion. We shan't be long, Vic. Say ten minutes—"
"No, I'll talk. Don't send her out."
"Certain?"
"Yes. I'll talk."
Vic turned back. She said, "It's not easy for a girl to know whether she's coming or going."
Bishop came closer to Petman. "They took Starling's body away. Who's they?"
"Craddock—"
"By car?"
"Yes—"
"Where to?"
"I don't know—"
"Where to?"
"The river—he said the river."
Bishop considered. It wasn't important, at this

moment, where the body was. He said:

"Who slung all the furniture out of this flat and shifted this new stuff in?"

"I did—"

"Who else?"

"No one else—"

"It was more than a one-man job, to do it as fast as that. Who else?" He came closer. Petman watched him. He said, turning his head away to deflect a blow:

"Caretaker."

"He's been paid well?"

"What do you think?"

"You didn't have long—two hours—before I told the police there was a dead man here. What was the set-up?"

"I don't know. It was Craddock's orders—"

"You don't want it known that Starling was killed. Why not?"

"I don't know—"

"Why not?"

"I—"

Bishop whipped his right arm back and measured the distance, skinning the man's jaw as the head swung with the mouth flapping open—"*I don't know*—God's truth I don't!"

Bishop said, "All right, we'll ask Craddock. Where is Craddock now?"

"I don't know—"

"Vic, this time you'll have to—"

"I dunno—you've got to believe me—I dunno where Craddock is!" It trailed off to a whimper. Petman had lost all his strength. All his strength was in Bishop's pocket, with the safety-catch on.

"We'll find him. Who killed Starling?"

The voice was going hoarse with giving the same answer.

"I don't know. Craddock and I came up to see him, and we found him on the floor—"

"How did you get the blood off the carpet? Come on, Petman—"

"There wasn't any blood—there wasn't a drop—"

"Was he shot? Slugged? Knifed?"

"There wasn't a mark on him, not a mark—"

"Sure he was dead?"

"He was dead all right."

"Who d'you think killed him?"

"I don't know—"

"Who do you *think*, Petman?"

"I haven't had time to—"

His throat blocked and he stared at the telephone. The bell was like another person in the room, suddenly yelling.

Bishop spun his glance back to Petman. "You expecting a call?"

"No."

"Answer it." He moved, with Petman, towards the telephone. "And listen. When you're talking, obey my signals, or I swear you'll leave here on a stretcher. Go on, pick it up."

Petman sniffed back catarrh, letting out his breath as he picked up the receiver. Vic was watching Bishop. His eyes flicked to look at her. He gave the smallest shrug, and looked back at Petman. Petman said into the phone:

"Who is it?"

Bishop levered the earpiece away from his head, by half an inch. The voice was clear enough.

"The Major. Are you alone?"

Bishop nodded. Petman said:

"Yes, Major."

"The Levinson girl—did she go to the police?"

Bishop nodded. Petman said:

"Yes, Major. They came here—"

"What happened?"

Bishop whispered. Petman said, "I put them off."

"They didn't believe her story?"

"No. Everything's all right here, Major."

"I expect that. You know what happens if anything goes wrong."

"Yes, Major."

"Listen. I want you to go to the Orient Wharf, in two hours from now—that is, at three o'clock. It's just below the Pool. You reach it through Scotsman Road. I shall be there, under the archway where the road leads on to the jetty. Repeat."

Bishop listened hard.

Petman said, "Three o'clock, under the archway where Scotland Road meets the jetty, at Orient Wharf."

"Scotsman Road—"

"Scotsman—"

"That's all."

The line closed. Bishop guided Petman's hand, putting the receiver back. He said:

"Get some clothes on."

"Where am I going? Listen, if Craddock finds out I've crossed him, he'll kill me—"

"I wouldn't blame him—"

"You can't do this—for God's sake listen—I let you off, didn't I? I—I didn't shoot—"

"You hadn't got the guts. Get some clothes on. Come on, Petman, we're waiting."

Petman turned and opened the door to the bedroom. Bishop followed him. As Petman cleared the doorway he swung round bodily and threw his weight at the door, slamming it. He was scrambling to lock it when Bishop hit it, as near as he could to the edge. The timber winced and a crack went down the paint. The second try got the door open with a crash as Petman lost his balance on the other side. He was getting up when Bishop came in.

"Come on, Petman. Get some clothes on. We're waiting."

16th
MOVE

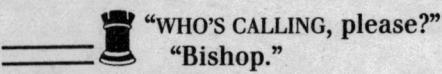

♜ "WHO'S CALLING, please?"
"Bishop."
"No, Mr. Bishop, the Inspector's not in his office."
"Has he gone home?"
"I shouldn't think so. Let me try Operations."
"Thank you."

He waited, keeping the door of the kiosk open with his foot. Outside, Vic stood with the gun steady. Petman leaned against the wall, smoking a cigarette she had given him. He leaned there, bored. He wasn't afraid of the gun. But he wasn't running.

"Operations—you're trying to find Mr. Frisnay, sir?"
"Yes."
"You're Mr. Bishop?"
"Yes."

"You happen to know Mr. Frisnay's middle name, sir?"

"Claude."

"That's right, Mr. Bishop. He's out in the G.P. car."

"I want to talk to him, urgently."

"I see. Where are you?"

"Near Wensford Close, South-west One."

"Just a minute, sir."

Vic took a few steps back, so that she could talk through the open doorway without turning her head away from Petman.

"Any luck?"

Bishop said, "Yes."

The Operations Sergeant came on again.

"Can Mr. Frisnay pick you up, sir?"

"Yes. Not here, though. I've got Petman with me. I don't want him seen. We'll be"—he tried to remember the area—"we'll be in the entrance to the Gents, at the end of this road where it joins Bridge Street."

"The Gents' Lav., sir?"

"Down the first few steps, out of sight. Tell Mr. Frisnay he can meet me at my convenience."

The Sergeant kept his voice straight.

"He'll be there, sir."

Bishop rang off and came out of the box. "We can go down parallel with this road, and cut through to the junction without being seen much." He took the gun from Vic and put it away.

Petman said nothing as they started off. He walked a few paces in front. Bishop said, "And don't forget. I can run faster than you."

The G.P. car slid in quietly to the kerb. Bishop saw its black roof through the railings. The radio antenna quivered to stillness. He said:

"After you, Petman."

Frisnay was out of the car. They came up the steps in single file. He looked at Petman and said, "Why did you bring him with you?"

"Every citizen has the right to arrest a man. I've arrested him."

"Charge?"

"Threats, while armed."

Frisnay said to his observer, "Put him in the car."

He got into the back, with Vic and Bishop. The doors were slammed. "Thomson, we'll drop this man at Cobb Street."

"Yes, sir."

They drove away, down Bridge Street. Frisnay asked:

"What happened?"

"Let's wait."

"All right."

Bishop went into the little station at Cobb Street, made the formal charge, and came back to the car with Frisnay. Frisnay said, "Cruise, area B."

"Yes, sir."

Bishop filled his pipe. Frisnay dropped the window an inch. "Right."

"When Miss Levinson found Starling's body," Bishop said slowly, working it out, "and ran out to my car, Craddock and Petman were somewhere near, either going toward Flat Nine or perhaps trying to follow Veiss. They found Starling, just as she did. They believed she was the only person who knew that Starling was dead—apart from his killer. While I was following Veiss they covered up."

"Covered up?"

"According to Petman, Craddock took the body and dropped it into the Thames. The caretaker must have had a suite of furniture stored—probably it was waiting to be moved into an empty flat, or had been moved out and was waiting for transport. They paid him to help Petman do the switchround—"

"In a couple of hours?"

"In two hours."

Frisnay watched the smoke from Bishop's *meerschaum* go skeining through the window-slit. "Trying to break down Miss Levinson's story. She was the only one who'd seen Starling's body . . . "

She said, "They nearly did it."

"M'm?"

"I had a job convincing you. I had a job convincing myself. For a while I thought I must have been seeing things."

Frisnay said, "I admit they came close to pulling it off. But you stuck to your guns too well."

Bishop said, "One of Miss Levinson's most attractive characteristics is adhesiveness. She always sticks."

Frisnay said, "Why didn't you phone the police, while Mr. Bishop was following Veiss? We'd have got there while they were still trying to do the switch."

Bishop said, "I told her not to."

"The smart type."

"I thought it better to get Veiss without a lot of fuss."

"You didn't get Veiss, and you nearly got killed."

"Don't hit me, I'm only young."

Frisnay grunted. Vic said:

"Why doesn't Craddock want anyone to know that Starling is dead?"

"It might be because he wants to keep Veiss out of Number One Court on a murder-charge.

He knows we're close. Once I can pull in Veiss, we have the Z.69. And Craddock hasn't."

Bishop re-lit his pipe. Frisnay opened the window wider and said, "I believe this is how they cure bacon."

Vic asked, "Why is Dr. Veiss on the run, Mr. Frisnay?"

"For the same reason. To keep out of Number One Court. He too knows we're getting close. He's running from us, from Craddock, from the Hutton woman and from you two."

They listened as a signal came through. It was not for the G.P. car. Locations were going in to base. In a moment Bishop said, "Was he running from Starling, too, when he killed him?"

"Did he kill Starling?"

"From what Miss Levinson says about his body, it seems possible that Starling's heart failed; and we saw Veiss leaving the flats. It looks as if Veiss was in Flat Nine, waiting for Petman to come in. For some reason—probably because he was setting out systematically to wipe out people who were in opposition to him—he dropped the man dead and left the flat."

"While I was phoning you," Vic said.

"Yes."

Frisnay stared ahead through the windscreen, between the driver and his observer. "You say that, according to Petman, Craddock dropped

Starling's body in the river. Does Petman know where he went from there?"

"No. I asked him. But they've arranged to meet."

Frisnay's head turned. "When?"

"Three o'clock this morning. Craddock rang up. I made Petman answer the call. I don't think the Major twigged."

"Where are they to meet?"

"The Orient Wharf, below the Pool."

Frisnay waited a few seconds and then said, "Tell me if I've got this wrong, Hugo. Is Craddock pin-pointed, time and place, ready for picking up?"

"That's right."

"You couldn't have mentioned this before, could you?"

"There's plenty of time—over ninety minutes yet—"

"I've got to mobilize half the Metropolitan—"

"Have you, Freddie?"

Frisnay waited again, then said, "All right, which way do *you* see it?"

"Craddock is quick, and he slips. He's been slipping us for some time now. This meeting is arranged at a tricky spot—a Thames-side backwater littered with warehouses, storesdumps, small shipping and derelict hulks. It's one of the most broken-down jetties on the stretch. I don't know how many men you've got at your disposal, or how many it will need to guarantee a water-tight trap. I should say it would take some organizing, by night, with only ninety minutes—"

"Hugo, you can't do it."

"It's the neatest way."

Vic was hunched sideways on the seat. She was shaking her head, watching him. Frisnay said:

"You can't sell it. You can't meet Craddock alone."

She murmured, "Hugo—"

"Listen, Freddie. You and the Assistant Commissioner sent me after Petman. I came back like a good boy, with the right change. What's different about Craddock?"

"You don't realize—"

"I'm not asking this because it'll pass the time for me instead of going to bed, or because I think I can do more than half the Metropolitan Police plus you and the Assistant Commissioner. I'm asking for a chance to get Craddock by taking him unwares. He's expecting one man there, to meet him. I'd be within a yard of him before he could duck—"

"But you—"

"I think it would save us all a lot of time. If I don't pull him in, you can take over."

Frisnay was silent. The car nosed down Brick

Street and turned back into Picadilly. They were round the Wellington Memorial before he said:

"Two conditions."

"They are?"

"One, that we throw a cordon round that area before you go in. Two, that you go armed."

Bishop tamped his tobacco down and fumbled for match. He touched Vic's hand, and pressed it, just quickly. He said:

"Yes to the cordon. No to the gun. It'd get in my way, make me nervous. I don't like loud bangs—"

"Suppose Craddock makes one—"

"He goes in for silencers—"

"That's no argument—"

"It'll have to do—"

"You're a damned fool—"

"Coconuts to you too, Claude." He got his pipe going.

Frisnay said with controlled impatience, "When do you start?"

"Soon. I'm going home for some strong black coffee first. I'll be leaving there in something like an hour from now. If you're organizing the cordon personally, pick me up on your way."

"I'll be there before you. I've got to check with the P.L.A. about shipping. Craddock might be down there because of something to do with Starling's body, if it's true he went there to sink

ROOK'S GAMBIT

it; but the Thames is on the route to anywhere. He might be taking a trip." He said to the driver, "King's Road."

The car turned left, off Knightsbridge.

Bishop said, "Well, I'll leave you to fix up your side. Vic, what about bed?"

"For me?"

"For you."

"I'm not sleepy." She tried to get the worry out of her voice.

"You can't come with me, this time."

Her face looked pinched, in the light that slid by from the street-lamps. She said, "I'll be around."

"Not alone."

"Mr. Frisnay will fix me a ticket—"

"Now look here, Miss Levinson—"

"I've helped you a great deal. You said so. Don't start getting mean."

Bishop said quietly, "Look after her for me, Freddie."

The car turned right, into King's Road. Frisnay said in a patient, stifled voice, "I assume Miss Levinson will be joining Mr. Bishop for strong black coffee. A police car will therefore call for Miss Levinson at Mr. Bishop's flat, at two-fifteen precisely. From then on she will be under strict police orders, so help her."

She smiled faintly. "You're quite nice when

you're being human, Mr. Frisnay. You must be wonderful off-duty."

"May the good Lord continue to preserve my ancestors in a state of heavenly bliss," Mr. Frisnay said.

The car turned gently into Cheyne Mews.

Miss Gorringe was wielding the Cona.

She said, "What's your deadline, Hugo?"

"Two-fifteen. I'll leave here when they come for Vic."

She put the Cona down and made for the door. "Any minute now. I'll get my coat."

He brought his head up. "You going out, Gorry?"

"Yes." She opened the door. He said:

"Where to?"

"With you, as far as the point where you leave the car—"

"Now listen—"

"I know all the arguments. I've heard them before, on these occasions. I can no longer sit here knitting my eyebrows while you race gaily about, throwing yourself under tube-trains and into the Thames."

Feebly he said, "You might gum up the works."

"Never have, have I?"

He said, "It's checkmate. Get your coat."

The telephone rang. He said, "Right, I'll take it." She went into the hall. Vic watched him as he answered the phone. "Yes?"

"Mr. Bishop?"

"Speaking."

"Sergeant Gray here, sir. Message from Mr. Frisnay."

"Right, Sergeant Gray."

"We've checked with the Port of London Authority. There's a Norwegian cargo-boat, the *Dornhaven*, sailing just after four o'clock from Pier Two in the Orient Wharf area."

"What does she carry?"

"Timber, but she's going back empty, except for a few crates."

"Will she be under surveillance?"

"Yes, sir, just to make sure."

"All right. Anything else?"

"No, sir. Message ends: If trouble, raise immediate alarm."

"Thank you, Sergeant Gray. I will. If."

He rang off and Vic said, "If Craddock's going aboard a ship—"

"I don't think he is—"

"But you think Dr. Veiss might be."

"Yes. That could fit. Craddock's traced him to that area might even know his plans. He wants help, from Petman. He arranges to meet Petman an hour before the *Dornhaven* sails."

Miss Gorringe came back with her coat. Vic said:

"Hugo, if Veiss is going to be there, as well as Craddock, you'll have to change your plans."

"Think so?" He didn't appear interested.

She stood close to him. "You must let the police handle this now, on their own. If Veiss is jumping a ship it means he's been driven out of the country, at last. He'll be desperate and he'll have the Z.69 with him. You wouldn't stand a chance, in the dark."

She knew it was no good. She glanced towards Gorry. Gorry shook her head slowly. She looked back at Bishop. "You must change your plans now, Hugo."

He was wandering out to the hall. "Sorry. But I must change my shoes. Tonight's a night for crêpe soles."

She said to Miss Gorringe, "I wish—"

"I know. But it's no good, Vic."

"You think there's going to be trouble down there?" She sounded bleak.

"Of course. Trouble is Hugo's natural destination."

"But this time he—he might be killed."

Miss Gorringe smiled tightly. "He might, every time. So far there's always been a next."

"But tonight you insisted on going with him, as far as you could."

"Yes." She put her coat on, tying the belt loosely.

"Why?"

"Tonight is different."

"You're uneasy."

"And you have a flair for understatement."

Vic said, "But we can't—" and stopped as Bishop came back.

"Gorry, where are my pipes?"

She eyed him patiently. "There are some in your pockets, I imagine. There are some on your desk. Don't look now, but there's even one in your mouth."

"Oh." He took it out, and found a match. She said:

"Relax."

"M'm?"

"Relax. You'll need your nerves, later."

He said briefly, "I'm perfectly relaxed."

She looked at his shoes. He had changed them. There was nothing more to do.

When the doorbell rang she went to answer it.

Vic said quickly, softly, "Hugo, don't go. Not alone. Leave it to them."

"I can't."

"You must."

"It's a one-man job." He let his pipe go out, deliberately, so that he could leave her to look for matches. He was impatient with her. They never understood, or even tried to.

She said, "I'll do anything you say. But don't go alone."

"Think with your head, not with—anything else. We want Veiss. We want Craddock. We want the Z.69."

"I only want to see you left alive."

He turned away, patting about for matches. He knew how bleak she looked, standing there in the middle of the room, watching him. They all looked like that when he—oh, damn! Leave it. They never understood. It was time they took the trouble to understand. Maybe one of them would, one day.

"Vic, the patrol-car's here for you."

"I'm ready."

She went down the stairs. Out in the mews, the police-car was waiting, its lights doused. Bishop said, "Vic, we'll all come back later and have a night-cap."

"Yes." She looked back once, as the car turned out of the mews, its rearlights flicking on, winking out of sight.

Bishop got into the Rolls-Royce and started the engine.

Gorry sat beside him. He put the gears into mesh.

"Poor kid," she said.

"She'll be all right."

"That's not what she's miserable about."

They turned into King's Road. It was two-twenty-one, by the dashboard clock.

17th
MOVE

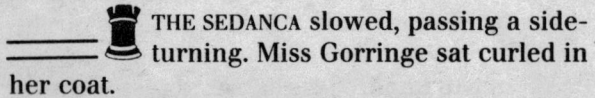

♜ THE SEDANCA slowed, passing a side-turning. Miss Gorringe sat curled in her coat.

"Robert Street," she said, "leading to Thurlestone Dock." She checked the book. "It'll be the next one, on the left."

The car swung silently into Scotsman Road. Cranes came up slowly against the skyline. The tarmac hissed under the tires but the air was clear of rain. Bishop passed a yard-way, pulled up and backed.

"You're going on foot," she asked, "from here?"

"Yes. Time-check?"

"Nine minutes to three."

He switched off the engine. "Look after the car for me, won't you?"

"I shall be here." In the same tone that she always used at a time like this. There had been so many times like this. She should have got used to them by now. But there was still the big moth, beating in her stomach. She said, "Good luck."

"Thanks."

He walked out of the yard into Scotsman Road. Twenty paces down he froze. For a moment he couldn't see the man.

"Just a minute, there."

A torch came on, dazzling him. Then it went out, leaving total darkness for a few seconds. "All right, Mr. Bishop."

Quietly Bishop said, "How far is the archway?"

"About two hundred yards, sir, across the railway sidings."

"You chaps here in strength?"

"There's a lot of us about, but you won't be stopped again."

"Good. I don't want to turn up late."

He walked on, keeping to the middle of the footpath that ran alongside the road. In the road there were chips of stone, droppings of coke, debris left by trucks passing in the day. It was easier, on the path, to go silently. As he walked, the cranes rose, skeletal above the horizon of shed-roofs. There was a slight zephyr, blowing from the river. That made it perfect.

"You're Mr. Brown, aren't you?"

"Yes, Miss."

She moved on the seat. A spring creaked. She said:

"You were in Wensford Close, earlier tonight, when we thought I'd mistaken the flat number."

"That's right."

She gazed through the side-window. "From here, where is the archway?"

"Not far. Behind those sheds, over—"

"Hello, KJ-9. Hello, KJ-9. Mr. Bishop has just gone through D-block. KJ-6 out."

She felt cold, still. She asked him, "Is that us? KJ-9?"

"No, Miss. That's the Inspector's car."

"Mr. Frisnay?"

"That's right."

They listened again, "All cars. All cars. Time two-fifty-eight. Unless urgent, no further signals. No further signals. KJ-9 out."

She said, "That was Mr. Frisnay, wasn't it?"

"Yes, Miss. That was the voice of the master."

She began to shiver, and tried to stop. After a minute, she managed.

"Gray, give me the glasses."

"Here, sir."

Frisnay stood against the car, bracing his left shoulder against the roof-line. The archway, the embankment, and the ground surrounding were deserted. The light was not good; but it would pick up anyone moving, anywhere near there.

He lowered the glasses.

"How's the enemy?"

"Minute to go, sir."

Miss Gorringe sat without moving. A cigarette was in her hand. The constable who had stopped Bishop had been to talk to her, just for a minute or two; but she hadn't been very co-operative. She didn't feel like talking.

She drew on the cigarette again. It was quite absurd to think of him not coming back. Just a slow walk down to the archway, a stroke of bad luck, and nothing more. It was always absurd to think of him not coming back, just as it was absurd to think that she herself could ever be run over or have cancer or drown. Because he was, and had been for so long now, a projection of herself, an indivisible, indispensable element of her life.

At least there wouldn't be any more pipe-ash all over the place.

It wasn't possible even to pretend to be funny. She threw the cigarette out of the window and took a deep breath. It wouldn't be long. This couldn't go on for ever. It never had, before.

"What do you think will happen?"

"That's anyone's guess, Miss."

"You're very calm." Better to say anything, however pointless, than to sit in silence, and wait.

"Wouldn't do to get excited, would it?"

"Does your job ever excite you, Mr. Brown?"

"Oh yes, when leave comes round." He turned his head. "Don't you worry. We shan't see any fireworks tonight."

"I'm not worried about us."

He looked away again. "Mr. Bishop knows what he's doing."

A tug hooted. The sound came fresh on the soft south wind.

"As long as he knows what the other man's doing."

"Ah, Major Craddock. Ask me, the Major's had it, this time."

The tug hooted again. She wondered why. There was no fog.

"Sar'nt Gray."

"Sir?"

"It's three. I think we'll get on to the running-boards now."

Gray climbed out from the observer's seat, shutting the door silently, not letting the catch click. Frisnay said to the driver, "Morris, if I give the word, drive at full-bore for the archway. You won't tip us off the running-boards, don't worry."

"Right, sir."

Gray and Frisnay stood with one hand secure, locked round the door-pillars. With his free hand, Frisnay raised the night-glasses again.

"Is it three yet?"

"Just on, Miss."

"If—if nothing happens, what do you do?"

The shivers began again. She clenched her hands, her whole body.

"Go on waiting till it does."

The tug had not hooted again. When it did, she would have to stop herself crying out. She couldn't remember, before, ever having had nerves. This was what it was like.

The clock on the dashboard ticked. Its regular sound was loud in the car. For something to do, she checked the panel. Water temperature was dropping from the nineties. The ammeter showed a half-amp discharge made by the panel light. The fuel-gauge showed seventeen gallons, nearly full. The rest of the instruments were at zero. She wished she had a book. She always wished she had a book at these times, and wished that he would let up a little and lose his taste for danger. She wished, too, that the Pyramids were round.

The clock on the dashboard went towards five minutes past.

She wished it would stop.

"Anything yet, sir?"

"Yes." Gray looked at Frisnay. Morris glanced up, through the driver's window. "A man, moving, half-way up the embankment." He braced his elbow on the roof of the car, to steady the night-glasses.

Morris put the gears into bottom, and switched the ignition on, and held the clutch out, and moved the handbrake off. Then he sat with one finger poised over the starter-button, left foot down on the clutch, right foot ready on the throttle.

Gray murmured, "Think it's Craddock, sir?"

The zephyr passed their ears, softly. They turned their heads, listening. Frisnay was immobile. The night-glasses were an integral part of his silhouette.

"Can't tell. Might be Mr. Bishop." A gust cuffed his face, bringing the Thames smell with it. "Moving down the embankment now. Making for the archway. Morris, are you ready to go?"

"Ready, sir." His finger itched against the starter-switch.

Sergeant Gray strained his eyes. He could see something moving at the foot of the embankment; or he believed, because Frisnay had said there was something there, that he could see it.

"Still coming down the bank. But I can't quite make out—"

They were some two hundred yards from the archway, so that, even with the breeze coming in their direction, they could not hear, for a few seconds, the explosion. They saw its flash, a bright orange flare bursting in the mouth of the archway and blossoming out to fierce yellow and then to white as the arch bulged, broke up, and collapsed. Then the sound came, buffeting their heads. Above the sound, Frisnay was yelling faintly:

"Morris—get there!"

18th
MOVE

THE CAR closed in with its acceleration taking it wide across the verge of scrubby grass and debris. The rear tires were still spinning for grip as the suspension flexed and bucked over the bumps, sending the engine's note to a scream and then bringing it down as the wheels found grip and thrust the car straight, plummeting for the pall of dust that had bellied out of the archway, out of the hole where the archway had stood.

As the brakes came on, third gear dragged the speed down on closed throttle. The car slewed, righted, slewed again, and then slid to a halt a dozen yards from the pile of rubble as Frisnay and Gray came off the running-boards and sprinted forward. The fringe of the dust came into their lungs and they began choking as they ran. Earth was crumbling, tumbling lazily down from the embankment.

Morris did not go with them. His left hand knocked the lamp-switch, and the headlights sent their beams stabbing into the dust-cloud, throwing the shadows of the two men against it. He tugged the receiver out of its clip and snapped the switch down: "KJ-9 to to all cars—KJ-9 to all cars—explosion at archway—archway collapsed. Black-out ends—we can receive signals. We can receive signals. KJ-9 over."

He remembered hearing a clatter, just as he had pushed the starter-button and gone away. The Inspector had thrown the glasses into the car. He fished about for them. They had landed on the floor, at the back. He checked them against the reflected glare on the dust-cloud. They were not broken. He sat calmly, bringing the immediate scene through the lenses in a slow level arc, from the left of the cloud as far as the railsheds ninety degrees away; from the right of the cloud to the roofs of the sheds ninety degrees round. He looked for a man running. He saw nothing.

Frisnay had stopped. He stood for a moment among the tumbled bricks, his eyes stung by the dust. It was no use poking about here. If anyone had been here, there was no hurry to find him. At the back of his mind—his trained police-mind that remembered he had to get Craddock—there was the thought of Bishop, buried and bloodied, somewhere here under this shambles of a tomb. He fought down nausea. He had known Bishop a long time.

Behind him KJ-4 came up, driving hard and stopping with a shudder of wheels across the edge of the debris. Its lights came on, doubling the glare. The dust was beginning to clear, to settle. Someone was getting out. Vaguely, as he moved again, climbing the embankment, he was aware of the small figure—the Levinson girl. She was asking someone what had happened, and where Bishop was.

"Gray!"

"Sir?"

"Search the bank on the far side!"

The Sergeant went clattering across the bricks.

Headlights brightened from Scotsman Road, playing fitfully on the scene and then fixing it as the sedanca stopped and Miss Gorringe got out.

"What happened?"

Morris called, "The arch blew up."

"Where's Mr. Bishop?"

"They're looking for him." He concentrated again on his radio. The air was jammed, asking for information and orders. There was no information; there were no orders. If Craddock was running, he'd run into them somewhere. There was nowhere he could run, and get clear.

Frisnay came down the bank at a loping trot, keeping his balance, dodging over the slope of rubble and running along the bank's foot at the other side.

"Gray!"

There was no answer. Gray was out of earshot.

Vic stood with Miss Gorringe.

"Can we do anything?" The words were sickly.

"I shouldn't think so. Don't worry."

"I'm not worrying."

It was too late for that. They could at least stop worrying now. Whatever had happened was over.

Men were running up from the water-side—night-shift workers, watermen, Thames-side crews, men with business in the Orient Wharf area, men without business there. They came shouting their questions. They received no answers.

The dust had settled, much of it drifting along the soft breeze and settling against the cars and the row of huts by the siding. Shadows were sharp, now, against the embankment and the pile of rubble, cast by the six headlamps.

Frisnay tripped and went headlong, scrambling up and swinging back.

"Watcher, Cock."

He bent over Bishop: Bishop was trying to sit up. Frisnay said, "Don't move."

"Why not? Nothing's bust."

"Sure?"

"Give me a hand, will you?"

Frisnay got him to his feet. Bishop said:

"That's more like it." He draped an arm around Frisnay's shoulders. "But I've got a headache."

Frisnay grunted. "You're lucky." He was furious with Bishop. The mad fool shouldn't have persuaded him. He was furious with himself. In great relief, one laughs, or is furious. The tension unwinds slowly.

"What a turn-up," said Bishop. He stopped swaying about, and took his arm away. Frisnay dragged it back round his shoulders and said:

"Come on. Home."

They walked along the foot of the slope, awkwardly. Miss Gorringe had seen them. She met them, with Vic, half-way between the embankment and the three cars.

"Hugo—"

"Hello, darlings—"

"Freddie, is he all right?"

"Why ask Freddie?"

Frisnay said, "Yes, he's all right."

"Where's ruddy Craddock?" Bishop's voice wavered. His left leg gave under him and Frisnay took a better hold. "It's Craddock we want—remember?"

"He won't be here."

"Why not?" Bishop stopped. Frisnay said:

"Gorry, lend me a hand. We've got to get this blithering fool home—"

"Why not?"

Tersely Frisnay said, "This was a booby-trap—"

"I don't see—"

"For Pete's sake be quiet. You've been bashed on the head by a brick."

Miss Gorringe said quickly, "Freddie, he's really all right?"

"Yes. Nothing broken. Just shock—"

"Whad'you mean, a booby-trap?"

They got him nearer the sedanca.

"Dammit I can walk! You goin' to let Craddock slip you?"

"He won't get through the cordon, if he's here—"

"Booby-trap—for me?"

"No, for Petman. It was Petman he was meeting here—"

"Petman." He swayed badly. They opened the door of the car. "But why did Petman—?"

Miss Gorringe said, "Hugo."

"Yes?"

"Be quiet, and get into the car."

He wiped dirt from his face. "All right, Gorry. All right."

Frisnay murmured, "Can you get him home?"

"Yes."

"I've got to look after this lot."

"Of course."

Vic asked her, "Can I—?"

"I'll need your help, yes."

Bishop said from the back of the car, more clearly than he had spoken before, "Freddie, what are you going to do?"

"Keep the cordon here till daylight and go aboard the Norwegian ship—"

"Search it?"

"Search the whole of the river. Now go home."

When the car had turned, and was driving away, he walked slowly across to KJ-9. "Give me the blower, will you?"

The booster whirred in the luggage-boot. He said into the phone, "KJ-9 to all cars. Switch to Plan B and give locations on arrival. Maintain outer cordon, concentrate on water-side." He paused. "Hello, River patrols. KJ-9 to River patrols. Over."

They came in. "Hello, KJ-9. Receiving you. Boat 5 over."

"Hello, Boat 5. We're going to Plan B and searching the *Dornhaven*. Please co-operate and search all craft in this section. KJ-9 out."

He gave the receiver back to Morris and got into the car.

He said, "Right. Operation Mills of God."
"The what, sir?"
"Just get moving, Plan B."
"Yes, sir."
KJ-9 moved off.

Miss Gorringe had opened the door quietly. In the dim light of the room her eyes registered slowly. The curtains were still drawn. Rain fell softly on the window-sill.

"Hugo." It was a whisper. The rain peppered the panes.

"Yes."

She jumped at the sound of his voice. He sat upright. He said, "Your nerves don't sound too good, Gorry. Didn't you have a good night's sleep?"

She crossed the room and sent the curtains racketing back.

"You imagine there's anything left of my nerves, after yesterday?"

He blinked gently in the strong light.

"What happened yesterday, then?"

She stood at the end of his bed, looking cool.

"Why, nothing. You got run down by a tube-train and then blown up by a bomb. Apart from that I nearly passed out with boredom. My nerves are perfect; as perfect as mincemeat can ever get."

He looked round for the papers, and said soothingly, "You exaggerate everything. Yesterday went off all right."

"With a bang, God knows."

"Where are the papers?"

"I didn't think you'd want them, at least until lunch." She left him. Chu Yi-Hsin squeezed elegantly through the doorway, sprang on to the bed, sat facing him, and purred. She had a purr like an aeroplane propeller just about to disintegrate by centrifugal force. It practically rocked the bed.

"Good morning, angel-face," said Bishop.

Miss Gorringe came back and dropped the morning editions on to the bed.

"Freddie hasn't phoned. You were going to ask that, next."

He brooded over this, looking at the Siamese. Miss Gorringe sat on the foot of the bed and eyed him obliquely. It was still odd, to see him here, gazing at Chu Yi-Hsin. How many lives did these two have between them? Eighteen?

"That means," he said, "that they didn't get Craddock. Freddie was saying something about a booby-trap. What was that to do with?"

"Petman."

He looked up at her.

"Oh yes, Petman. Tell me more."

"Craddock rang Petman and told him to be

under the archway at three o'clock. As far as Craddock could know, Petman would keep the appointment."

He nodded slowly. "Ah. So at three o'clock sharp the balloon went up—"

"And the archway came down, leaving Petman still safe in custody and you spreadeagled under the night-sky, sucking a brick."

He opened the papers restlessly.

"What about Craddock? It was Craddock we all wanted."

"All Craddock wanted was Petman dead."

He dropped the papers.

"Something is beginning to stir in my turgid subliminal. If Craddock wanted Petman blown up, it could mean he was thinking of doing a scarper. Yes?"

"It could."

"And wishing to leave no evidence of his nefarious affairs behind him, he set out to effect that. So we spiked his guns on that score, if Petman's still alive. That is at least something." He lay back on the rumpled pillows. "What happened to little Vic?"

She reached for a cushion, from a chair, and dropped it behind his shoulders as he leaned forward. She said:

"Little Vic went home with her nerves held together by bits of string."

He gazed at the cat. "She's a honey."

"Is that American for something?"

"Yes. Means a dish. The more I see of little Vic—"

"Hugo."

"M'm?"

"Take care of her. She'd bounce hard if you finally disillusioned her."

He didn't look at her. "Why should I?"

"Women fall in love through a telescope. You jump in with your eyes shut. Did your mother ever remember to tell you about being kind to little girls?"

He said irritably, "I have been warned. Your solemn duty has been discharged."

Levelly she said, "It's not my duty. But I like that girl, as much as you do, in a rather different way."

He looked at her in a moment. The irritation had gone.

"What would I do without you, Gorry?"

"You'd carry on just the same, but it wouldn't be fun for me."

They listened. The Siamese lifted its head. Bishop said:

"I've got a ringing in my ears."

Miss Gorringe got off the bed, calling over her shoulder:

"Shall I switch it through?"

"Please."

He waited until the ringing had stopped, then picked up the bedside phone, and said:

"Good morning."

"Congratulations."

He got his brain clear. He said:

"Thank you, Georgina."

"I would have missed you."

"So did Craddock."

He put out his right hand, and stropped Chu Yi-Hsin efficiently behind the ears. The purr threatened to wreck the bedsprings.

"Was it Craddock who mined the archway?"

He said, "Well, I don't know, really. It might have been Jamboree Night at the Cockle-pickers' Slate Club. You know how some people never know quite when to draw the—"

"Can I see you, Hugo?"

He hesitated, then said, "That would bring charm to my morning. Here, or where?"

"Wherever you are."

With a wicked leer in his tone he said, "Wonderful. I'm in bed."

"Did the bomb hurt you?"

"Made me sneeze a bit, but then I'm allergic to brick-dust."

"So you weren't right under the archway."

"If I had been, my insanitary remains would have been plastered all over the Orient Wharf."

"I'm glad they're not."
"Well yes, I am, rather."
She said, "I'll be round in—how long?"
"Half an hour. Join me for eggs and bacon."
He put the phone down, eased the Siamese off his legs, and went to have a shower. It would be nice to see Georgina again. Today, it would be nice to see anyone again.

Frisnay said to Sergeant Flack, "I'm seeing the A.C. at twelve, so I'll need results by then."
"Yes, sir."
"Does Petman know what happened last night?"
"I don't expect so, sir. He won't have seen any papers—"
"Then tell him. Go down there now and tell him yourself."
Flack moved for the door. "Right, sir. Then question him about Craddock?"
Frisnay looked at his calendar and said:
"No. Not yet. Just make sure he knows that Craddock meant him to be blown to hell. Let him brood about it for a couple of hours; then I'll go down and pump."
"Right, sir."
He went out and shut the door. One of the telephones was ringing. Frisnay picked it up.
"Yes?"

"Morning, Freddie—"

"Hello, lad. How d'you feel?"

"First rate. Didn't get Craddock, did you?"

"No. He couldn't have been there. If he had been, we'd have winkled him out."

"You search the *Dornhaven*?"

"We had it searched. The captain had a lot on his mind for some reason, but his ship was clean, and we let her sail."

"I think Veiss was there."

Frisnay gave his calendar a very old-fashioned look and said:

"You think what?"

Bishop said, "I think he was trying to get out of the country, with or without Craddock, certainly with the Z.69. For Craddock, there was one loose end: Petman knew too much. Petman had to be dead before the *Dornhaven* sailed."

Frisnay lit a cigarette, interested. But he said:

"Craddock hadn't much to worry about, once he'd cleared the Channel."

"Except for Interpol. And Petman could have tripped him. Are you going to grill him, and tell him what a nasty mean man Mr. Craddock was, to—"

"Yes, in a couple of hours. Look, can you come round, so that we can work this over more fully?"

"Not for a while, Freddie. Miss Hutton is expected for elevenses."

Frisnay squinted hard at his cigarette.

"Where," he asked, "does she come in?"

"I shan't know, until she's talked. On the phone she sounded very pleased with something or other. Maybe herself. But she didn't ask to come round just to tell me how many more eggs Granny can suck without blowing her corsets. Will you be in your office after lunch?"

"In the building, somewhere."

"I'll find you."

They rang off.

Frisnay stared for some time at his calendar. In three days he was due to go on leave. He wondered what his chances were. He put it roughly at about a thousand to one against. They didn't know where were Craddock was. They didn't know where Veiss was. They hadn't got the Z.69. They hadn't pinned the Thorburn killing on anyone. They hadn't found Starling's body, after dragging the Thames half the night. A thousand to one against. That was being optimistic.

Bishop played boogie. The cat watched the keys. She sat on top of the piano, her amethyst eyes barely open. She was purring. Bishop could just about hear what he was playing. He couldn't hear the doorbell at all.

Miss Gorringe got up from behind her desk.

"Would that be Georgina?"

"Would what be?"

Miss Gorringe went out to the hall. He was aware that the bell must have gone. It was, yes, probably Georgina. He began playing *The Lady is a Tramp*.

Miss Gorringe came back. She said from the doorway:

"Hugo—Miss Hutton."

He swung round on the stool, looking delighted.

"Thank you, Gorry." Miss Gorringe went out. "My dear Georgina, you look ravishing."

She wore an apple-green travelling-suit with a loose coat. A striped scarf was tied with perfunctory perfection at her throat. She placed her I. Millers neatly across the carpet, smiling.

"Hugo, you look well." Her tone was surprised.

"You sound disappointed."

"Just a little astonished."

"Then I'm disappointed. I hoped you might be glad."

"I'm glad Craddock didn't kill you, with that thing."

"But you wouldn't enter a convent if I fell down an elevator shaft by accident." He crossed to the sideboard. "What will you drink—bitter aloes?"

"Nothing for me." She sat down on the davenport. He said:

"It is a bit early, isn't it? How did you know I nearly got snatched upwards by the angels last night?"

"I heard the explosion."

He raised his eyebrows, tucked his chin in, and said:

"Oh." He leaned carefully against his desk, watching her. She really did look ravishing today. Prussic acid dressed up as a posy of passion-flowers. "So you were down that way yourself. What were you doing—seducing a stevedore on Wapping Steps?"

"I was waiting for Dr. Veiss."

He began feeling edgy. He was one jump behind, so far.

"Waiting for Dr. Veiss? and he—er—didn't turn up?"

She smiled tightly.

"Yes, he turned up."

"This is madly interesting."

She nodded, taking out a cigarette. "Yes, I thought it might be." He picked up the desk-lighter and flicked it for her. "Thank you."

He put the lighter down and said:

"I'm dying to know: how is Dr. Veiss these days?"

"Still alive, so I believe."

"You treated him gently, then?"

"Not very. He was unconscious when I left him."

"Overcome by your fatal charm."

"No. Blackjacked."

He felt more and more edgy. His head must still be full of brick-dust. He couldn't fit anything in. He couldn't jump ahead of her, mentally. He didn't know the answer, yet. He ought to be selecting one of several.

He said amiably, "Poor Veiss! And this was—where?"

"Somewhere on the fringe of the police cordon."

"That's quite a large area."

"He was trying to reach a ship."

"The *Dornhaven*."

"Yes." She wasn't surprised that he knew. He wasn't one jump ahead of her, even psychologically. She knew all the answers, this morning. He hadn't even seen all the questions, yet. She said, "The Major had fixed it for Veiss to go on board, an hour before she sailed."

He thought: my God, it came close, last night. Craddock, Veiss, and the Z.69 had nearly cleared the country.

"I see," he said. "And Petman?"

She studied her cigarette. "Petman was too good. He was too loyal to the Major."

"He was therefore placed in a position of absolute trust, until he was no longer required."

"Yes."

"That would have been at three o'clock this morning."

She nodded. "Yes. I'm sorry he missed that appointment. I never liked Petman."

"M'm. He had banana-colored guts. That wouldn't have appealed to you."

She said, "Where is he?"

"Petman? In the hoosegow, thinking dreadful things about the gallant Major."

"He knows that bomb was meant for him?"

"I understand he's being informed. For obvious reasons." He glanced up from the desk-lighter. She wasn't rattled. Nothing, this morning, would rattle her, he decided. This morning she was ravishing and unrattlable. It made him feel more edgy than ever. She was in complete command now. Why?

"I suppose he'll squeal on everyone concerned."

He said, "Well, that's the general idea. It's not a bad way of getting information."

"It doesn't matter. It's too late."

Complete command. He thought: How?

"What a shame! Petman will be so disappointed." He kept the worry out of his voice. He didn't like the way this was going. He said, "Suppose Petman tells them that when Starling died, he—"

The phone began ringing. He didn't finish what he was saying. It might help him, to talk, first, to whoever was calling him up. It might be Freddie.

He murmured, "Excuse me." He put his hand on the receiver.

She said, "Hugo, don't answer it."

This morning, she could give orders. Why?

"Don't answer it?" He held the receiver. "But it might be my lobster-monger, to ask—"

"It might be your friends at the Yard. I don't want you to talk to them, yet."

Yet. What was that odd word doing there?

He drew her claws out, by putting the receiver to his ear. He was just going to say hello when he saw the thing she was holding. Now he knew. This was why. He looked at it, and got his voice straight, holding the receiver away from his ear. He could hear Vic's voice, coming faintly out of the phone.

"Put it down." Georgina said.

He said, "Don't think me inquisitive, but what's that thing you're holding?"

"This is the Z.69."

He was aware of his watch ticking on his wrist, and of Vic's voice, saying hello.

"It's the pretty girl," he said, "with dark hair. The one I brought back from Madrid. I'd like to tell her I'll ring back. Can I?"

"Yes." It would make her feel good, to allow concessions. "But be very careful."

He put the receiver to his ear and said:

"Hello, Vic."

"I didn't think you were going to answer. Are you all right?"

"I'm fine, but can I ring you back, soon?"

"Y-yes. I just wanted to know how you were this morning." She sounded rebuffed.

"I'm in good fettle, and I'd love to talk to you, as soon as I can."

"It doesn't matter. As long as you're all right."

Gorry had talked sense. Vic was beginning to hurt easily.

He said, "I can't talk for long now, because the place is surrounded by Indians and the shanty's ablaze. But I promise I'll phone you."

She sounded a little better. There was a smile in her voice. "All right, Hugo."

"Bless you," he said, and put the receiver down, and leaned against the desk again, and looked at the Z.69. "Not much of a size," he said, "is it?"

"Made for the handbag."

It was the shape of a cine-camera, the size of a small-caliber gun, with a gray-flecked finish. A glazed aperture at the end of the little tube might have been a lens of some kind.

He said, "You—er—you've read all the instructions, I hope?"

"Instructions?" She put her cigarette into an ashtray, without moving the Z.69.

"I mean, you know how it works?"

"Oh yes." The smile was chilling. "There was a sparrow perched on my window-sill this morning. When I opened the window it flew on to a fire-escape at the side of the next building. When I used this it dropped straight down. I heard it hit the ground. Death appeared to be instantaneous."

"How happy that must have made you feel." He tried to keep the edge on his voice.

"It gave me a thrill."

"I can imagine."

"With this I can do anything."

"Almost."

"Anything."

He said after a moment, "It's your move, Georgina."

"Of course. I have plans, for us both. If—"

The door opened, after a light knock. Miss Gorringe came in and said, "I've made some coffee. Would you like it in here, or shall I—"

"Gorry."

"Yes?"

He turned his head. "That little number in gray is the Z.69."

Miss Gorringe looked at it. She said:

"My, my. And we've been searching for it almost everywhere, haven't we?"

"Almost," he said. "Except in Miss Hutton's hands."

"Shall I—bring the coffee in here?"

Georgina said, without looking away from Bishop, "I'm afraid we haven't time, Miss Gorringe, but thank you."

"Not at all. If you'll excuse me, I'll—"

"No. I'd rather you didn't. Please close the door and sit down where I can see you."

Miss Gorringe hesitated, and glanced at Bishop.

He said, "We're in check."

She shut the door and sat near it.

"No, over there, please. Nearer Mr. Bishop. Then I can see you both."

When Miss Gorringe had moved, Bishop said:

"All right, Georgina, so this is it. You've got the Z.69. The big dream is yours, and Craddock has lost. You haven't come here just to show off the new toy. So?"

She said, "Craddock hasn't lost until I've cleared England; perhaps not even then. He's a considerable fighter. At the moment he's not certain that I've succeeded in getting hold of this—"

"But he has an idea—"

"He has an idea."

"So you're on ice."

"The phrase will do."

"But with that in your hands," he said, "Crad-

ROOK'S GAMBIT

dock can only lose. Either the trick or his life, now."

"He knows I wouldn't spare him if he tried to stop me getting clear. But to fire this at him, I have to see him, first."

He took out a pipe, and reached for the tobacco jar. She said, *"No."* His hand froze. "Use your tobacco-pouch. It's softer, when thrown."

He got his pouch, filling the pipe, saying slowly, "So Craddock will remain invisible, until one day when you turn your back for a second..."

"Not one day. There's just today. Before tomorrow I shall be gone."

"I see. Where is he now?"

"I don't know."

He found a match, and struck it. "You never will, until it's too late." The blue smoke clouded up. The little flame leapt. She watched it. She reminded him, with her steady gaze, of Chu Yi-Hsin. Their eyes were equally beautiful.

"It won't be too late, Hugo. I'm leaving England."

"That's silly."

"Why?"

He dropped the match-end into the ashtray on the desk. It was a heavy jade bowl. He wondered about it, for a second or two.

"Hugo, you'd be dead before it reached me. This thing is very quick."

He said, "One has to amuse oneself by mental exercise."

"Your brain's keen enough, don't worry. Why shall I be silly to leave England?"

"Well, what's the point, Georgina? Veiss is still alive, or so you believe. I've no doubt you tried to finish him off, but failed. I imagine you didn't have any time to do more than seize the Z.69. And while he remains alive, the thing can't be exclusive to whatever government you'll get to buy it. And even if Veiss is dead, or dies, or for some reason cannot or will not reconstruct this design, his department will have the data, at Kingston-Electric."

She smiled thinly. "That's being taken care of."

"Taken care of . . . what a discreet phrase that is. And your passage from England—how will that be taken care of?"

"You'll go with me, as far as Paris. After that I shall vanish. If you're co-operative, you'll come back safely."

"Thank you very much."

Miss Gorringe was smoking a cigarette. She was spending her time measuring distance, methods, and chances. She was also ready to pitch in if Bishop began a brawl by throwing a desk or anything.

Georgina said with care, "The first thing you must realize is that I'm prepared to kill you instantly if you don't co-operate in every detail."

"With me dead, you—"

"With you dead, I'm still not finished. I still have this, and a hope of getting clear with it. But you won't throw your life away. You have too good a time. And it'll be much easier for me to leave the country with you than without. And much more fun."

"Don't let's get sentimental, sweetheart. You've not a hope in hell, with or without me. Both the Yard and the Special Branch have put a security watch on docks, airports, and the Golden Arrow. No one would stop me, but they'd stop you. You, Veiss, and Craddock are at this moment the prisoners of England. Sorry it sounds so romantic, but it's really the case."

"Not really. Craddock and Veiss, yes. Not me. I have the ace. This."

He re-lit his pipe. If Vic called, to see why he had been so odd, on the telephone, there'd be a chance. That was about the only one. Freddie was busy, until after lunch. Craddock might show up. That would be interesting.

"Yes, you have the ace. I shall be wide-eyed with wonderment to see how you play it."

"I'm glad. Because you'll be with me." She looked at her watch, lifting her head swiftly. He had not moved. She said, "You'll please telephone Frisnay and say that you're taking me out of the country for reasons that you can't, at this stage, reveal."

He had started to smile. Her tone went thin.

"You'll assure him that by doing this you'll speed up the case, and get Craddock, Veiss, and the Z.69."

"Have you finished?"

"For the moment."

"Then there's only one snag."

"Well?"

"Dear old Fred don't never believe in fairies."

"He trusts you, and he trusts your judgment, because you've never let him down. I know that, because you must have persuaded him to let you keep that rendezvous at the archway last night. If you could do that, you can do this. Don't worry, Hugo, you'll be able to persuade him."

"I'm delighted you think so. It puts you in clover, surrounded by false hopes. And what about the Major?"

"As far as the airport we shall have police protection, because you'll tell Frisnay, quite truthfully, that Craddock will try to stop us leaving England. If they see him, they'll take him."

"They will, I agree."

"You can put that argument to Frisnay."

"Argument?"

"That we shall act, partly, as a decoy, to help them get Craddock."

"I see. That might persuade him, certainly, unless of course he's remembered to screw his head on when he got out of bed—"

"It's up to you. You'd be stupid, wouldn't you, not to try?"

He inclined his head. "All right, I'm your man. But you'll forgive me if I leave instructions with Miss Gorringe to phone the Yard as soon as we leave here, and tell them the situation—"

"Miss Gorringe is going into the country, just for the day. There's a car and chauffeur calling for her. She'll be treated with all respect, providing she gives no trouble."

He smiled again, and said:

"You feeling in the mood to give trouble, Gorry?"

"It might be entertaining."

Georgina said: "I'm quite certain the situation doesn't escape either of you. You're both in my hands, completely."

"When does the car call for her?"

"In two hours, at one o'clock. By that time you'll have persuaded Frisnay—"

"What if he won't listen?"

Viciously she said, "He'll listen or you'll lose your life, remember that. Mine's already in jeopardy, and to me yours is much cheaper. Until I land in Paris I'm balanced between disaster and magnificent success. You'd be a fool to provoke me."

He looked at the ormolu clock. "The car calls for Miss Gorringe at one. And then?"

"Our plane leaves at two-twenty. I've made the booking, and we shall travel light. If you don't do anything stupid, you'll be back here by this evening. So will Miss Gorringe." She paused for two seconds. "If either of you makes a mistake, you won't see each other again."

They froze as the doorbell rang. It caught them in odd attitudes: Miss Gorringe with her cigarette half-way to her mouth; Bishop with one hand raised to smooth his hair back; Georgina with the Z.69 half in one hand and half in the other as she began changing it over.

She said in a moment, when the bell had stopped:

"Have you any idea who that might be?"

"Might be Mr. Sylvester, dropping in for a quick sloe-gin."

She said with her eyes cold, "Are you expecting anyone?"

Bishop said nothing. Miss Gorringe said:

"Not really. Someone rang a little time ago. Did you answer the phone, Hugo?"

"Yes. It was Vic."

Miss Gorringe smiled sadly at Georgina. "We can't help you, my dear. It might be anyone, from the minerals man to the Assistant Commissioner of New Scotland Yard."

The bell pealed again.

Georgina said, "They'll go away."

"Probably. I wonder who it is. Craddock?"

Her eyes flickered. She was scared, then, of Craddock. He said:

"Or Frisnay. This is interesting. I mean, our Fred's a busy man. If he's ringing my bell, as might easily be the case, he might not get back to the Yard until any old time, and I shan't be able to tell him our bedtime story over the phone. Meanwhile, planes are taking off for Paris with monotonous regularity, and Major Craddock is taking his time—"

"Phone him," she cut in.

"Craddock? I don't know his num—"

"Phone Frisnay."

The doorbell rang again, a long one, a final one. He said, "But that's probably Frisnay, at the door."

"Phone his office; then we'll know."

He said slowly, "Very well." He put his hand on the receiver. The receiver wouldn't travel far, because it was wired to the instrument. The instrument, which was heavier, and therefore more attractive as a missile, wouldn't travel far either, because it was wired to the wall-point.

"Hugo. I'm very nervy today. I'm liable to fire this without thinking, if I'm startled." She watched his hand. "Don't startle me."

"What you say is quite true, Georgina. That's why I've behaved like a good boy, so far."

"Keep it up, and we'll all be happy."

He picked up the receiver and dialled Whitehall. While he was doing this, she said levelly:

"If you get hold of him, you know what to say. You've thought of this new plan, of taking me out of England. You're certain it'll succeed. You can't see him about it because you're pressed for time."

He listened to the ringing-tone. He murmured obediently, "Mr. Bishop regrets cannot see Mr. Frisnay because is jet-propelled."

The Yard answered. He said, "Inspector Frisnay's office, please."

He waited. She said, whittling every word cleanly, "You know the real score, Hugo. You have to convince Frisnay. The alternative is that you're found dead of heart-failure."

Sergeant Flack came on the phone and said:

"The Inspector's not in. Can I take a message, sir?"

"Not really, no. When d'you expect him back?"

"I can't say, Mr. Bishop."

"Well, I'll try again later."

He put the receiver down, and looked across at Georgina. "The Inspector is not in." He glanced deliberately at his wristwatch. "They don't know when he'll be back." His eyes met hers again, and noted how frozen they were. "I do hope this delay won't impose too great a strain on you."

19th
MOVE

FRISNAY TURNED the corner of the passage and met Sergeant Flack.

"Miss Levinson's waiting in your office, sir."

"All right." He would get her out. He didn't want to talk to any women this morning. He wanted to sit and think. Before lunch he had to find a way out of this deadlock. They'd all been beating the air too long. The Chief hadn't put it quite like that. Not so politely.

Flack added, "She's got Dr. Veiss with her."

Frisnay looked at him. "Veiss?"

"She says she picked him up, sir."

He gazed at Flack. "She says she picked him up," he repeated, trying to make sense of what Flack had said. Two hundred men had been looking for Veiss since he had been missed from home. Miss Levinson said she'd picked him up. Before breakfast, or just while she was doing her nails?

He nodded, going towards the door of his office. Flack said, "And Mr. Bishop's rung twice, at twelve-fifteen and again at twelve-thirty. He said he'd like to talk to you urgently, sir."

"I'll ring him." He went into his office. Miss Levinson was leaning against the filing-cabinets with her hands in the pockets of her coat. She looked pale and red-eyed, but her voice was bright enough.

"Hello. Mr. Frisnay."

"Good morning, Miss Levinson," He looked at Veiss. Veiss was slumped in the big leather-covered chair, his eyes closed. He might have been asleep. He gave no sign that he was aware that Frisnay had come in. He looked dead-beat. She said, straightening up and coming towards Frisnay:

"He's still rather weak. He needs a rest."

They spoke quietly. "Where did you find him?"

"I was poking about along the water-front, early this morning. I'm covering the story officially now, and I hoped I might pick something up in the Orient Wharf area, now the hunt had died down."

Frisnay sat down at his desk. There was a man on Pier Two, another at the rail-sheds, three more along that stretch, and a handful of Special Branch men combing for scraps from Blackfriars to beyond the Pool. Why hadn't they found Veiss?

He said again, "Where did you find him?"

"In a dockside café, being looked after."

He offered her a cigarette. She shook her head. He said, "Have you had any breakfast?"

"A bun."

He pressed a bell-push. "How did Dr. Veiss get there?"

She perched on the arm of the smaller chair.

"He was attacked, last night or early this morning. When I found him, his memory wasn't very good; but I think it's coming back by degrees."

A constable knocked and put his head in. Frisnay said:

"Organize some sandwiches and coffee, will you?"

"Right, sir."

The door closed. Frisnay asked, "Did you bring him straight here?"

"Yes. I thought that was best."

He looked at her with a polished teak face. "You're quite a worker, Miss Levinson."

She looked demure. "I aim to please, Mr. Frisnay."

How could they look like little angels, and do these things, and still go on looking like little angels?

He looked at Veiss. His eyes had opened. Frisnay said:

"You've had a nasty time, Dr. Veiss."

"Yes. Yes." He sounded bewildered.

Frisnay spoke gently. "Do you remember who attacked you?"

"No." The white hands rested along the old dark leather of the chair. The pale face was turned to look at Frisnay, the head lying against the chair-back. "It was in the night. In the dark. I did not see."

"Why do you think you were attacked?"

"I do not know."

"Was it robbery?"

"I do not know."

In the same gentle tone, "Dr. Veiss, where is the Z.69?"

"It is lost." The face seemed to collapse, becoming older.

Frisnay said in a moment. "The motive for the attack was, in fact, robbery. You'll appreciate, of course, that you'd be advised to answer my questions, Dr. Veiss. I won't ask many, until you feel more rested."

Veiss said nothing. He watched the window behind Frisnay, as one does in a dentist's chair. Frisnay said:

"What does the Z.69 look like?"

"It is small. It is gray."

"How small? The size of a small revolver, or—"

"Yes. It is gray."

"Miss Levinson," Frisnay said, "What's the name

of the café where you found Dr. Veiss?"

"The Tin Kettle."

"In the Orient Wharf area."

"Yes, about five hundred yards down-river from the archway in Scotsman Road."

"Thank you; that's accurate." He snapped down a switch and spoke into the microphone. "Operations."

"Operations, sir."

"Get a car along to a café called the Tin Kettle, five hundred yards down-water from Scotsman Road, North Bank. Standby there, and stop anyone leaving the café or going into it. Get their names and enquire their business. Sergeant Flack will arrive soon after you do."

"Yes, sir."

Frisnay closed the line and looked as Flack tapped on the door and came in.

"I was tuned-in, sir."

"Go down there. You'll need a warrant for search." He slowed his speech. "You are looking for an electrical instrument the size of a smaller revolver, grey. There's a chance it's been concealed there, somewhere in the café." He felt Veiss's eyes on him, but didn't glance that way. "If necessary, rip the walls down, pull the roof off, and dig over the foundations. You know what I mean."

"Yes, sir."

ROOK'S GAMBIT

"If you find this thing, handle it with great care. You're looking for the Z.69."

Sergeant Flack looked shot, said simply, "I see, sir." He turned to go out. Veiss said weakly from the chair:

"I did not hide it. It was lost. They took it."

Frisnay said, "That's all Sar'nt Flack."

Flack went out. Frisnay said to Veiss:

"We have to think of everything, you understand."

"But I tell you—"

When the telephone nearest Frisnay's left hand rang, Veiss seemed to cringe at the sound. Miss Levinson came over to him and touched his hand, smiling.

"You can have a good rest, soon," she said.

He tried to smile back.

Frisnay said into the phone, "Yes?"

"Freddie—Hugo."

"Sorry I was out—"

"That's all right." Frisnay thought his voice sounded very case-hardened this morning. "Freddie, I've got an emergency plan on, with not much time available." There was a pause. "I'll need your help. If you'll help, it'll get us Veiss, Craddock, and the Z.69."

Frisnay looked carefully at Veiss. He said:

"Go on."

"I can't go into details. You'll have to trust me.

I'm taking Georgina Hutton with me on the two-twenty plane for Paris. Craddock will try to stop us leaving. We'll need your escort as far as the plane."

Frisnay said, "Have you been drinking?"

"For a start," Bishop said, "You'll bag Craddock, because he'll be desperate to stop us. You see, he thinks Georgina has got the Z.69."

Drily Frisnay said, "How'd you know he's not right? Someone's got it."

"Of course he's right. She's got it here with her. The first thing I can think of is to get her out of the country with it, with a full police escort, under your nose. Have you been drinking?"

Frisnay said impatiently, "What makes you think we can get the Z.69 if we let you do this?"

"Various factors. There's no time to tell you. You'll have to trust me, Freddie."

"Look, just how serious are you?"

"As serious as life and death. When did I last let you down?"

Frisnay looked up as Dixon came in with a tray of sandwiches and coffee. The girl took it from him.

"Hugo, I'd listen to you, but for the one thing. Dr. Veiss is here in my office."

"It doesn't surprise me. He was attacked, last night, along the River."

"What else do you know?"

"A great deal. It's because I know Veiss has lost the Z.69 that I've made this plan. You've got Veiss. You'll get Craddock before my plane takes-off, and I'll guarantee that I'll get you the Z.69." He said it again, putting his weight behind every word. "I guarantee that, personally."

Frisnay looked at Veiss. Miss Levinson was biting into a cheese-sandwich and stirring her coffee. He said finally:

"I'd have to see you, before you left the airport."

"Can't be done, Freddie."

"No deal, then. Sorry."

Bishop paused for a moment and then said, "Hold on, will you? Someone's bashing my door down."

Frisnay levered the receiver away from his head, to give his ear a rest. Miss Levinson looked at him over her cup.

"Please give him my love," she murmured.

"I will." He heard Bishop's voice saying hello. He put the receiver back and said:

"Yes?"

"All right, I can just make it, if you can come round within fifteen minutes. But I shan't be able to give you the full picture, even then."

Frisnay said, "We'll be round."

" 'We?' "

"I'm bringing Dr. Veiss with me, and Miss Levinson, who asks me to give you her love."

Bishop's tone broke step and then steadied as he said, "Thank her for me, and give her mine. What's she doing there?"

"She brought Dr. Veiss in."

"She's a bright little thing, isn't she?"

"Yes, she is."

"Bring her, but why bring Veiss?"

"I want to compare notes. This thing is ready to blow skywards and I don't want a slip-up."

"All right. It's a quarter to one. Make it five-to?"

"Five-to."

He put down the phone.

She said through her sandwich, "We going to see Hugo?"

"Yes."

The color was back in her face. He said, "But finish the coffee."

"I have."

"I admire your nerve, Georgina."

"There was nothing else to do. Frisnay must co-operate. If he won't do it without seeing you before we leave, then he must see you."

He happened to glance at Miss Gorringe. She smiled and said, "It'll be quite a party. And me in my apron."

"And me with my trousers down."

Georgina said, "I'm glad you realize you're both in a bad position."

"I've only got to make one sign to Frisnay . . ."

"You can't, without my seeing you. I shall be watching you all." An extraordinary softness came into her tone, breaking it down. "Hugo, don't let anyone get killed. It's going to be up to you."

He felt worried, about that, about the way she said it. She was prepared to kill, and she wasn't going to like it, any more than she had liked talking to him in the second-hand bookshop, so near to what had seemed his death.

He said, "You're serious, aren't you?"

She nodded. "Yes."

He said, when they heard the doorbell ringing, "It's five to one."

Miss Gorringe got up. "Shall I answer the door?"

"Please. I shall be just here, in this doorway, where I can see you. You'll please open the front door and then turn away at once—at once—and call over your shoulder for Frisnay to come in. Walk past me, into this room, leaving the door open. This has to go very smoothly. Shall I repeat anything?"

"No. It was perfectly clear."

She went out of the room, leaving the door wide open. Georgina watched her. She said to

Bishop, "Please move a little to your left."

He moved, and saw her in the long mirror beside the door.

"Thank you."

He thought there were five, maybe seven paces between them. If she gave him three seconds, he would try it. Two seconds could mean a sparrow's death.

She said, watching Miss Gorringe walk towards the front door, "It'll be fun, the Paris trip, and afterwards."

"Think so?"

She said, "Yes. I've got a letch for you."

"You choose an odd time."

"Not really. I'm excited. I'm on the edge of the big pit. But I'm not dizzy. It excites me, fiendishly. So I think about you, too."

He saw Miss Gorringe opening the front door. He murmured:

"There isn't going to be any Paris."

"Yes, there is."

Miss Gorringe called over her shoulder, "Come in, Freddie." She came back through the hall, and into the room. Frisnay shut the front door, and followed her with the others.

Little Veiss looked bewildered, and pale, and quiet. Vic looked across at Bishop, and smiled quickly. He moved towards her. Georgina said clearly, "Hugo, may I have a light?"

She was sitting in the chair, near the door. Her coat was draped over her folded arm. He bent over her with the table-lighter, and murmured, "You stage-manage very well."

The end of the cigarette glowed.

"Don't muff your lines, Hugo."

He turned away, glancing quickly at Vic, trying to say hello in the way she wanted him to say it. He thought she understood. He looked at Frisnay and said:

"Oh, Freddie, you've not met Miss Hutton." Frisnay was watching Miss Gorringe, who had seemed about to murmur something to him. Bishop said, "Georgina, this is Detective-Inspector Frisnay. Miss Georgina Hutton."

They nodded. Miss Gorringe was maneuvering, moving closer to Vic. Bishop passed her, to close the door. "Too dangerous, yet."

Nobody else heard. Vic and Frisnay had sat down. Veiss was on the davenport, sitting dejectedly. Bishop said:

"Would anyone like a drink?"

"You said you were in a hurry." That was Frisnay.

Bishop said, "That's perfectly true, Freddie. Can I have your decision?"

"No, not yet. You'll have to tell me more than you have so far. How d'you know Craddock thinks Miss Hutton has got the Z.69? How d'you know Craddock hasn't got it himself? Given answers, I'm prepared to fit in."

Bishop stroked the heavy jade bowl on his desk; but when he glanced up at Georgina, he could read her eyes. She was safe, here, with so many people about. The Z.69 was worse than a machine-gun in the room. He smiled faintly and said to Frisnay:

"No answers. Trust me."

"I trust you, but I've got to know more. There's an appalling risk attached to this thing."

"Yes, Freddie."

Frisnay looked across at Veiss.

"Dr. Veiss, would you please tell Mr. Bishop the capabilities of the Z.69?"

Veiss stared round him. "The capabilities?"

"What it can do."

Veiss spoke automatically. "It is a device transmitting a ray over distance, like a television transmitter. The ray is lethal. It has only to strike the little finger, or any part of the body, to kill instantly. It causes immediate mutation of the body's electricity, generating internal shock round the region of the heart. The ray is silent, and invisible."

Bishop was watching Georgina. Her smile was quiet; it was not triumphant; it was satisfied. He felt cold in his stomach. He said to Veiss:

"What's the range of this thing?"

"The range is limited only by the curvature of the earth."

"So you see, Hugo," Frisnay said, "it can massacre a crowd of people, in the instant. Someone has the Z.69 at this moment. Whoever it is must be handled with extreme care. Now you see what I'm driving at, why I'm reluctant to let you go? Suppose this trip causes an accident?"

In the silence, the bell shrilled. Veisse brought his head up. Bishop looked at Gorry. He said:

"One o'clock."

"Yes."

Frisnay said, "One o'clock?"

"I'm driving into the country, for the afternoon. That'll be the car, calling for me."

"Freddie, before she leaves, can we have have your decision? Do I catch the Paris plane, or not?"

Frisnay said nothing. Georgina said:

"You'll have to go, won't you, Miss Gorringe?"

Frisnay switched his glance to Georgina, and back to Bishop. He said:

"I'll play it your way. For a time. I don't guarantee how long."

Bishop waited. It wasn't for him to say whether that much would suffice. The silence drew out. Georgina got up from her chair, leaving the coat draped over her arm. She was smiling at Bishop, so he said, "All right, Freddie."

Miss Gorringe opened the door. She turned.

"Have a good trip."

"See you for dinner."

"It's a date."

She went out, saying good-bye to the others. Bishop watched her go. Frisnay said, "Use your phone?"

"Do."

Georgina watched him dialing three nines. When he was through, he said, "Operations, Inspector Frisnay. Get this to Sergeant Gray. Miss Hutton and Mr. Bishop are leaving in a few minutes to catch the two-twenty plane for Paris. Lay on immediate escort, V.I.P.I. coverage. Inform Special Branch. Spare car to pick up Dr. Veiss and return him. Detailed orders by signal when escort assembled. Queries?"

"Return Dr. Veiss to here, sir?"

"Yes."

"All clear, sir."

Frisnay put down the phone and looked at Bishop.

"Your move."

The man was thin, tall, graying, had a stoop, a pleasant voice, hard eyes, looked like a lawyer. He closed the front door for Miss Gorringe. She asked:

"Is this the car?"

ROOK'S GAMBIT

"Yes, Miss Gorringe." He opened the driver's door for her. "I've been given to understand that you drive."

"I do."

"Then I shall sit at the back, so that I can watch you."

"I'm flattered." She got behind the wheel of the Jaguar. "What's your name?"

He spoke from behind her. "Parker."

"You seem well-mannered, Mr. Parker. Times have changed. Thugs used to be tougher than you are."

She was trying to think what she could do, most easily, without provoking him. Wreck the engine, if she could, before they had driven too far. Snap a con-rod by hammering away at crawling speed in top. But these rods were going to be hard to snap. Parker was saying politely:

"The courteous approach is not necessarily a sign of weakness, Miss Gorringe. I should perhaps advise you that you are, regrettably, seated with your spine exposed to a loaded firearm, and that I have my duties to—er—discharge, should you force me. I do hope, however, that our drive into the country will be undisturbed by any incident."

"I can't promise not to crash my gears." She started the engine. "Which way do I go?"

"Turn left, and take the Mitcham road, across Chelsea Bridge."

She botched the gears deliberately, to give plausibility to any further mistakes she might make.

"Don't shoot the driver. She's doing her best."

Bishop said, "What about the escort, Freddie?"

"It'll pick us up before we've gone a mile." They stood in a small group, near the front door. Georgina was slightly away, watching them. "Now that I've fixed things up, can you give me a clearer picture?"

"Well—I—"

"Time's too short, Hugo, isn't it?"

Georgina said it smiling. Frisnay gave her a glance and said to Bishop, "I'm putting my complete trust in you. I hope you're not putting your trust in Miss Hutton."

"Not by one inch."

She said, "Thank you, gentlemen."

"Let's not make any bones, Miss Hutton. We know who you are. You can't get your hands on the Z.69 and you won't let Craddock. You're clearing the country and giving us Craddock on a plate. If the situation is less simple than that, I'm relying on Mr. Bishop to know the rest. He believes it'll help us if you're allowed to leave England. All right, you're leaving."

She said coolly, "Whether you pick up Craddock or not?"

"Whether or not?"

"No strings?"

"It's not our policy to make any promises to enemies of the State; but until I decide otherwise, you're free to go." He turned to Veiss. "Dr. Veiss, you'll be taken back to New Scotland Yard to receive whatever medical attention you need and to rest until you're recovered. Have you any objections?"

"No. I have no objections." Vic was holding his arm. "I will be glad, now, to rest."

"Then we'll go." He opened the front door. "Miss Levinson, we'll drop you wherever you say, if it's along our route."

"Thank you, it is. Just as far as the airport."

She followed Frisnay, helping Dr. Veiss. Georgina murmured:

"Hugo, you'll keep in front of me, always. This coat will be over my arm, all the time. The thing fires through cloth."

"It's such a nice coat."

"You've such a nice back."

She followed him down the stairs.

The car for Dr. Veiss had arrived. Frisnay guided him towards it and told the driver, "Take Dr. Veiss back and fix him up with medical attention. He's to be held, with amenities, until I'm back from the airport."

"Yes, sir."

Vic stood against the wall, where the small bay-tree stood in its tub. The light, reflecting from the white wall, touched the car with the soft glow that snow makes. Veiss looked as pale as a child watching from a window when there is snow on the ground. Vic lifted her hand, and he smiled to her as the car drove off, a smile so forced that she would rather he hadn't seen her at all.

She joined Frisnay. He was talking to his own observer. Bishop and Georgina were together, getting into the gray sedanca. Vic said, when she could interrupt:

"What's the exact situation, Mr. Frisnay?"

He turned to look at her.

"How does it strike *you*, Miss Levinson?"

"Miss Hutton seems to be in charge of this maneuver."

He nodded. "That's right. Please get in." He opened the rear door for her, then walked across to the Rolls-Royce. He said to Bishop:

"You won't see me until you reach the airport, Hugo. Maybe not even then. So have a nice trip."

"Thanks."

Frisnay was looking at Georgina, through her window that was half-way down. She looked very good in the car. Its lines suited her. She looked as if she had breeding. Frisnay said:

"England expects this day to see the last of you."

He turned towards his own car. Bishop's engine started up. The sedanca moved over the cobbles, and turned out of the mews. Frisnay sat in the back of the G.P. car and said to Brown:

"Give them a minute."

"Right, sir."

"Any signals come through?"

"Only locations, sir."

Frisnay said, "You comfortable, Miss Levinson?"

"Perfectly. Why can't we go?"

"If Craddock sees Hugo and that woman surrounded by police, he won't take a crack at them. But when he does, we'll be there." He leaned forward. "Give me the blower." He was feeling confident about this operation. Miss Levinson had brought Veiss in. Bishop was with Hutton. There was only Craddock to get. Put Veiss, Craddock, Petman, and Hutton in one basket, shake it up, and the Z.69 would drop out. That would be the lot. Then he could go on leave.

He talked into the phone, "Inspector Frisnay calling Bishop-escort—Bishop-escort. He has just left Cheyne Mews with Hutton in the grey Rolls, proceeding to airport. We expect Craddock to intercept—Craddock to intercept. If he does, he will be taken by any means short of shooting to kill. Come in with locations. G.P. over."

He passed the phone back to his observer. The

first one was already coming through:

"Hello, G.P. Going north along Sloane Street, Bishop fifty yards ahead, three cars between. J-5 out."

Frisnay said, "Start up."

"Sir."

"Hello, G.P. Waiting by Knightsbridge Tube. Bishop approaching from Sloane Square now. We are starting up, to proceed ahead of him. J-9 out."

Frisnay said, "We'll go now."

"Yes, sir."

The black Wolseley moved off, turning into King's Road.

"Go through the Park. We'll pick them up at Marble Arch."

"Yes, sir."

Frisnay took the phone, waiting until a location had come through—"Hello, G.P. Turning west along Piccadilly. To wait for Bishop, corner of Park Lane. J-3 out."

Frisnay said, "G.P. to all cars—all cars. G.P. heading through Park to join escort at Marble Arch. Maintain loose formation. Locations in five minutes. G.P. out."

He sat back. The thing was running. It was very like making a good gambit in a game of chess. Except that, in chess, only the King was in danger.

20th
MOVE

"STRAIGHT ON?"

"Yes. Across the bridge."

The Jaguar changed down, imperfectly, catching the lights at green and speeding up between the columns of the bridge. There had been no real chance, yet. But she would find one.

"How's my driving, Mr. Parker?"

"Very good, Miss Gorringe. It looks like being a most pleasant journey."

"With a safe return?"

He leaned forward. She saw the image of his hat in the driving-mirror, and heard that his voice was closer. "My instructions are to return you safely this evening, in time for dinner."

"But how civilized. I'm to dine with Mr. Bishop?"

"I've heard nothing to the contrary. I understand Miss Hutton will be leaving him when they reach Paris. It's a short journey home for him, and the plane services are frequent." His voice and his hat receded as he sat back. "I should like to think of you having an excellent dinner together this evening—you and Mr. Bishop."

They ran off the bridge on to the wider road, the tires singing. She said:

"You sound more like a godfather than a gunman."

"Oh please, Miss Gorringe. Certainly I'm an expert marksman, and various aspects of my career have not been quite in line with lawful custom; but I hardly consider myself a gunman. Turn left here, please."

"Left."

"We go through Clapham Common—a pleasant green foretaste of the countryside to come."

She drove more slowly, imperceptibly more slowly, as the figures dropped round on the speedometer trip.

"Let me pull up, Mr. Parker, so that you can come and sit in the front with me. The view would be nicer for you."

"The line of your neck is delightful, Miss Gorringe. Besides, that is where the hole will be drilled, in the event of any little mistake. Forgive my directness, but I thought perhaps a reminder might prove timely. Women are forgetful, and forgetfulness, at a time like this, is only one step short of oblivion."

She swung right, going across the common. He said in a few minutes, "And please go a little more quickly, or we shall be charged with loitering."

She pressed the throttle open a degree. With this man, it was going to be difficult to make a deliberate mistake; but it would have to be made soon, before they reached the open spaces and there was no help available.

The fuel-gauge read three-quarters full. There was no hope there. If she could reach forward under the dash, and find the thin copper pipe to the oil-gauge, and break it, would the oil come pumping out of the break, exhausting the supply until the bearings ran? She didn't know enough about these things. And he would see the oil, flooding the carpet in the front of the car. He would in any case be watching her hands, her every movement.

They pulled up for traffic lights. When they flicked to green, she left the handbrake-lever half-way on, so that the shoes were just rubbing. How many miles would it take for the red-hot drums to seize?

Towards Mitcham they began threading through medium commercial traffic. The smell was distinct inside the car.

"Miss Gorringe, I think you must have left the hand-brake on. Perhaps you'd see to it."

She released the lever.

"I'm sorry," she said.

"It was a pity, yes. But I doubt whether it would have done the trick in time. We're not going much farther than the suburbs."

"G.P. to all cars. G.P. approaching Northolt in D position. Maintain present formation. Hello J-3—J-3. Fix on green Windover saloon. Has been with us for some time now. Keep checking. G.P. out."

He passed the phone back.

"Are you going to let Mr. Bishop board the plane, Mr. Frisnay?"

He smoothed off his face to polished walnut. "We act according to circumstances."

"Do you think Craddock will show up?"

"If he believes Hutton has the Z.69, he'll show up."

"He's leaving it late."

"He can't do much on the main road. The airport's his best chance."

She watched the street unravel. They had not seen the grey sedanca, once, since Cheyne Mews. She had been looking out for it all the time. If she could have seen it, only once, a glimpse, she'd feel better, for no reason at all.

"How much danger is Hugo in?"

Frisnay said, "About as much as he always is. He spends most of his life kicking impatiently at death's door."

She accepted a cigarette. He lit it for her. She said in a little while, "Why does he do it?"

"I've never asked him."

"Would a psychologist know?"

"A psychiatrist might."

"You think he's crazy?"

"Not in the accepted sense. I'd just say he was a few yards round the bend. But he always seems to know the way."

"One day he'll lose it."

"One day we all do."

A signal came in. "Hello, G.P. Green Windsor saloon checked and cleared. J-3 out."

Frisnay, "I hoped we'd got a bite." He sat in silence for a mile and then said to his observer, "Nearing airport. Formation concentrate."

"Yes, sir."

The switch snapped.

Along the smooth twin-track the sedanca fled with perfection. The only sounds were the whisper of tires and the soft air-stream past the windows. Georgina was sitting as she had been when they had left Cheyne Mews, half-round in her seat, her coat doubled, the Z.69 out of sight. It would be easy, otherwise, for Bishop to bring his left hand down and deflect the ray, and wreck her chances before she could do anything.

He said, "Craddock hasn't got our trail."

"I'd like to think so."

Her nerves sounded in her voice. They were hanging on to the cliff-edge all the time. Their atmosphere was inside the car, as raw as cigarette-smoke. Her nerves were everywhere, emanating from her as if physically.

"But you don't think so?" he asked.

"No. Craddock's not far away. You don't know him."

"Nervous?"

"Why the hell should I be nervous? I'm holding the Z.69, aren't I?"

He pulled out, passing an articulated truck. He said, "And the moment you lose it, you're lost."

"Anyone who tries to get this thing will be dead before he starts."

"The death-rate's going to be high. A lot of people want the Z."

Viciously she said, "It's their own responsibility. They know the terms."

"They might not abide by them. Craddock certainly won't. Does he really think you've got the Z?"

"He knows I'd never leave the country without

it. And he knows I'm leaving the country."

"Did you tell him?"

"D'you imagine I've got suicidal tendencies? He knows, because he always knows the things I do."

"Then I don't think you'll get clear."

"Why not?"

"Too much against you. You're alone, against the rest. And you're not strong enough."

She said nothing. He could feel her nerves, fluttering in the air. He said in a moment:

"I had an illusion about you. I suppose I have about most beautiful women. I thought, for a time, that you were redeemable."

"I am." She spoke now with bright control, to show him she wasn't afraid. "I'm joining the Salvation Army, as soon as this is over."

He smiled faintly, thinking of her in a bun and bonnet.

"They wouldn't have you, sweetheart. They only take nice girls. And this won't be over, for you, for a long time. I'd say about fifteen years."

She tried to answer, with something brittle, but it blocked her throat. He felt sorry for her. They were beginning to burn her up, those nerves in there. He said, "At this stage, when you haven't killed anyone, I think they'd only deport you. That is, if you're not British by naturalization. You could leave for the Continent, free. Next summer there'll be roses, all over France. Down through Italy, with the sun hot over the vineyards, they'll—"

"Don't look now, Hugo, but you're getting desperate."

"But the moment you kill, or attempt to kill, or anyone dies because of you, the roses die and the sun goes out. After fifteen years, or whatever they give you for whatever you'll do, you'll come out an old woman, less than forty. Two years of Holloway takes four to live through. Twice fifteen is thirty. Have you ever been celled-in, for any time?"

"If I don't make Paris, it'll be because I'll die."

"If that's the choice you've made, I'm sorry."

"Are you going to get more and more desperate, the nearer we go to the airport?"

"Before this evening, Georgina, you'll have reached the end. Probably the end of your life. Certainly the end of your connection with Craddock and the Z.69. It'll be all over, except for the flowers, or the turning of the key. By this evening." He looked at the sky, through the side-window. "The sun's already on its way down, past the zenith. Going down towards evening. And you're throwing down your last cent to win a million. There's nobody to help you, except me."

"I can almost believe in you."

"Picture it: you're surrounded by police. Craddock is closing in. You're travelling with a man—that is myself—who will trip you up at any second. There are going to be a lot of seconds, a lot of chances, for me. If I were looking at your position, without bias, I'd say you hadn't a hope of seeing Paris for a long time, if ever again. You've got about fifteen minutes, now, to think twice. You see, we can get this thing from you, if we try hard. We're not worried about that. There's only one of us worried about you."

"I'm not worth it."

"No one ever says that and means it. We all think we're worth something. Most of us are right."

"I'm too caught up in this. I can't back out now."

"You can. All it'll cost you is a chance in a thousand of making a million. They're big figures, but they don't add up to much?"

"Do they really think you can talk me out of it, as late as this?"

"No. But you're more ready to listen, because your nerves are at breaking point and inside you there's a whole lifetime of living, crying out for a future."

"If you don't think it's any good, why talk?"

"It'd be on my conscience if I didn't. By this evening someone'll say to me: she didn't have a chance, did she? I'll say, no. But I'll be able to think: but I offered her one."

"How sickly can your sentiment get?"

"I'm trying everything. It's like having your eyes shut and poking around for the right bell-push. So far, they're all out."

She said nothing for minutes. When she spoke, her voice was steadier. "Thank you for trying. It might have worked."

"It might, yet."

"No. It's too late now."

"Is this Mitcham Common?"

"Yes. We turn off soon, and go to Lower Coulsdon. It's the road to the right, just beyond the bridge."

"Thank you."

The dry, hot smell from the brakes had gone. The engine was running perfectly. She couldn't, by the behavior of the car, hope for a breakdown this side of Hong Kong; and they weren't going much farther than the suburbs. It would have to be done soon.

He said, "It's the turning on the right. The cross-roads."

"Yes," she said. The mirror was blank. Fifty yards ahead of her there was a lorry. She considered ramming it, by accident, and letting matters take their course; but it wasn't certain that she'd win herself a chance to run. He would tell her to drive on, fast, if the damage weren't much; if it were, the impact might stun her. It was better to hit something with a known speed of zero, like a wall or a tree. There could be room for a certain degree of planning, if sufficient factors were known beforehand.

"Slow now; it's not far."

She said, "This is the bridge?"

"Yes. There's the cross-roads. We go right."

"I see."

The car took the bridge without slowing. There was the delightful sinking of the stomach as the gravity changed.

"You must slow down, or—"

"Yes, I'm slowing, Mr. Parker."

The acceleration was very good. The machine had been designed with that kind of thing in mind. It was well into the forties and passing the cross-roads with the engine feeling its head.

"Miss Gorringe. I have warned you."

His voice was close. She could see part of his hat in the mirror. "Slow down."

"Yes, Mr. Parker."

They hit the fifties at the beginning of the long road across the common and she kept her foot down, climbing to sixty and slapping the horn-press for gangway while Parker shouted from the back seat, "Stop the car!" She felt the metal press against her neck. She called:

"It's running away with me—"

"Stop the car!"

They touched seventy and she was leaning on the horn-press nearly all the time, weaving through light traffic, cutting a van close, hearing a snatch of the driver's yell as the windstream whipped it away. Parker called something; she kept the horn blaring, part of her mind on the road, part remembering how Hugo had told her to do it, how to pile up a car without singeing the eyebrows. That was the phrase he had used, laconically. It had seemed comic then. It seemed very earnest now.

Parker was calling, "You have two seconds, before I shoot."

The gun was jabbing into her neck.

"What are your chances, at seventy miles an hour with a dead driver? Do be serious, Mr. Parker!"

He was trying to climb over the back of the nearside seat into the front. She jazzed the wheel about to get his heart into his mouth so that he'd have something to chew on while she was busy. He stopped trying to clamber into the front seat. A car went past the other way, skinning their front wing and raising hell on its horns.

They climbed the hub of a lorry and cut-in,

gouging out a space between it and the car ahead, with the brakes dragging the pace down to a lurching fifty. The horns of the lorry blared a long note; the driver of the car in front was looking round, making no attempt to clear the road. It was a built-up area; he was already doing forty; he saw no reason to speed up or hug the ditch.

Parker said, "The moment you stop, I shall shoot, before you can get a message to anyone. Those are my orders, and my fee is high."

"If I stop, you'll shoot?"

"Yes."

"Then I'd better turn her over, and spoil your aim. You any good in a deliberate smash? Because I've had training—"

"You'll kill us both!"

"If necessary. Throw the gun down, where I can see it. Those are my terms."

"It's too late—"

"Throw it down, you damned fool!"

He kept it pressed to her neck. She watched the shape in the mirror. It was dodging about satisfactorily. When it began overtaking, the bell cut in. She said:

"That's a police-car. Throw down the gun."

"If you stop, I'll shoot. You know who's got the Z.69."

She couldn't argue. The plane had to take-off

for Paris, with the Z.69 on board. It was as simple as that. This man would shoot and run, and risk it. His fee had been high.

The police-car was alongside. There was nothing, for the moment, ahead. She braked suddenly. The black saloon overtook hard, with the crew waving for her to pull up. She let it gain a dozen yards, then flicked a look at the speedo-reading. Plus sixty-five. It was a useful speed. Below forty, you bounced back from a telegraph-pole, crushed to death. Above forty, you started to have a chance of snapping it and getting clear.

She kept her eyes open for as long as she could and dragged the wheel hard over. It wasn't easy to do. Every instinct dragged the hands the other way. Hugo had said there was only one thing to do, after turning the ignition off. That was to relax. She turned the switch an instant before the front tires screamed as the steering cocked over; then she tried to relax her muscles. That, too, was difficult but it was something to think about during the nightmare.

The car went over with a flick, coming half-round in an abortive slide and losing grip as one front tire ripped off the rim. Then it was sliding, with the sound of all the souls in hell screaming for mercy as the metal roof skated over the tarmac roadway. It travelled thirty yards, drifted towards the camber, and spun round, plummeting into the ditch and ploughing between the earth banks, showering turf into the air.

The police-car had stopped. Both doors were wide open and the crew was sprinting hard. One man had a fire-extinguisher in his hand. Three or four cars were pulling up, signalling in panic as the road became choked. People left their cars, running for the ditch where the Jaguar lay, cocked over.

The car-crew reached it.

"This door's free—get it open."

"She's alive—"

"Get this door open, for God's sake—"

"All right—you're all right—we'll get you out—"

"You'd better," said Miss Gorringe, "I'm in a hurry."

They dragged at the door. "You're in a hurry, all right."

Glass shattered, falling away like hailstones into the pool of petrol that was forming on the torn earth. She came out with her shoes off and one arm bright with blood.

"Hold that man—he's wanted—"

"What?"

"Hey, Jack—he's got a gun!"

"All right, he's flaked out—"

"Where's your car?"

"Eh?"

"I want a signal sent!"

The pool smelt pungent. "This lot's liable to go up—get her clear, and get this bloke out, quick!"

"I want a signal sent—"

"Signal? Who to?"

"I'm on the Craddock search."

"Craddock?"

She picked out the black Riley from the other cars. People were milling round.

"Hurry, will you?"

They had pulled Parker out. They put him on the grass, clear of the wreck. One man straightened up and said to her:

"The Craddock search?"

"Yes—you must have been alerted—"

"Car's up here. Come on."

He took her arm, clearing a way through the people. She said, "Can you get North London patrols direct?"

"They'll relay." He reached inside for the phone, and put the switch down. "Hello, BX—hello, BX. Stand-by, urgent. Over."

He said to her, "What's the signal?"

BX was answering, standing-by. She said:

"Can I? It'll save time." She took the phone. "Hello, BX. Message to Inspector Frisnay, patrolling vicinity Northolt Airport. Frisnay—Northolt Airport. Georgina Hutton is carrying the Z.69.

Hutton is carrying Z.69. Message ends. Repeat, please. Over."

She waited, getting her breath. The repeat came back.

She said, "Word-perfect."

The driver took the phone from her. "We're at present attending car-smash, Mitcham Common. Passenger armed with gun, but all under control. We need an ambulance. BX-5 over."

When he had finished reporting, he put the phone back into its clip and found Miss Gorringe sitting on the grass bank, trying to tidy her hair.

"Are you hurt much, Madam?"

"Not much. How's Charlie-boy, over there?"

"He looks bad."

"He was born bad. Will that signal go through all right?"

"Straight away."

"That's all I'm worried about, then."

The police-driver looked at the smashed saloon, the limp form of Parker, and the channel of ploughed earth along the bank. He looked back at Miss Gorringe. "Is that all?" he said.

21st
MOVE

AN AIRCRAFT was in the circuit, lowering, under-carriage down. From that height the twin-track road was a pale rut running through the green, and vehicles moved slowly.

They watched the plane, from behind their windscreens. The cars were spread out, with J-9 leading, half a mile ahead of the gray sedanca. Between the sedanca and the trailing man—J3—there were four other saloons. The G.P. car was in the middle of the string.

Vic said, "This is the airport?"

"Yes." He felt very alert. The decision still had to be made. He might let Bishop board the plane, with Hutton. If he did, there must be immediate contact with Paris by telephone. He said to Vic, "I must warn you, Miss Levinson, that you're here at your own risk. If anything happens—"

"If anything happens, Mr. Frisnay, I write it up for my front page."

He grunted. "Or they write it up for you, in the obituary columns." He leaned forward. "Speed up. We go through the gates behind Bishop."

"Yes, sir."

The G.P. car drew out, overtaking J-4. There was no acknowledgment from either driver.

Within a hundred yards of the gates they picked up the Rolls-Royce, and tucked in behind. The speaker buzzed.

"Hello, G.P. Hello, G.P. Signal from South London Operations. To Inspector Frisnay, patrolling vicinity Northolt Airport. Georgina Hutton is carrying the Z.69. Hutton is carrying the Z.69. Please acknowledge. JT over."

Frisnay's face splintered. He said to his observer:

"Acknowledge. Repeat signal, ensure all cars take it." He sat back, folding his hands, watching the rear of the elegant gray sedanca as it swung towards the gates of the airport. Vic said:

"That's why she's in charge."

"What? Yes. That's why."

She didn't speak again. He was thinking hard. There had to be a switch. How had South London found out? He spun his brain round and picked out two answers. Either Gorry had known, and had been under stricture, until a few minutes ago; or Craddock was slipping them all a fast one, anonymously. He decided to act on the first theory. It fitted in so well: Bishop's refusal to explain his plans, Hutton's appearance of authority, her decision to leave England. She wouldn't go without the Z.69. She'd got it, all right.

He leaned forward.

"Give me the blower."

The sedanca slowed.

"Park over there. Not too close to any other cars."

Bishop said, "There's not much of a gap, anywhere."

"Use the biggest one. Remember you're strictly under my orders."

He swung right, and came in a half-circle, choosing a gap between an Allard and a Landrover. He nosed in, and turned the ignition switch.

"All right here?"

"Yes." Her tone was tense. Her body was rigid. He was aware almost palpably of the thing under her coat. "Hugo, I'm getting out first. When I'm out, you follow. For your own sake, be careful."

She looked at him once. Her eyes were large, the pupils distended with fright. If she loosed off the Z.69, it would be in panic. He hoped no one would be in the way. He said:

"All right. You get out first."

She pushed open the door with her left hand. As she stepped on to the concrete, Bishop heard the car come up. It came up very fast, and braked alongside. He thought it was a police-car closing in. Her body seemed to spin round, but she wasn't hit. Her coat swung up. He caught a glimpse of the gray device, and then Craddock blocked his view. She was screaming something.

Bishop came round the car, swinging on the headlamp to pivot him. His run took him hard into Craddock, but Craddock spun free and stood with his feet astride. Georgina was on the ground, her hair over her face. She was cursing softly in her throat. Bishop was between her and where Craddock stood. Craddock began backing towards the Allard as a patrol car came up fast. He said to Bishop:

"Don't come for me."

The Z.69 was in his hand. His face was expressionless. The patrol-car had stopped, leaving dark streaks of rubber on the concrete. Men got out. Other cars were closing in. Bishop saw Frisnay. Craddock was standing still, his back to the Allard, his left hand on the door of the car he had driven up in. It was a hard-top XK-120.

He called to Frisnay, "Keep back. This is the Z.69."

Frisnay had got his men in a ring. It was clearly a predetermined course of action. There was no gap, anywhere. Inside the ring of men were Craddock, Bishop, and Hutton. She was getting to her feet. She began walking unsteadily towards Craddock, then Bishop stopped her, catching her by the wrist. She swung round. Her eyes had a killing look. She had lost her reason, for a moment. Bishop said:

"Steady up. There's nothing you can do."

She swung back, looking at Craddock, but did not try to wrench herself free of Bishop. She stood there calling Craddock a filthy name, over and over again.

Frisnay said, "Craddock, you've got to get through this cordon. Is there going to be any trouble?"

His tone lacked conviction. They all heard it. This was a try-out, to draw Craddock.

"There will be no trouble," Craddock said.

"You can't kill the lot of us, before we take you."

"I can. Don't force me."

An aircraft was taking off. They listened to it. Craddock jerked his head, but didn't look up. He said, "If I wanted to, I could bring that plane down, just by turning this on it. You know that, or should. I can leave these men of yours on the ground, for dead, and walk away. This weapon is more powerful than a battery of machine-guns. Bear that in mind."

A man moved, somewhere along the cordon. Frisnay called:

"Hold off, that man!" He looked round the cordon. "Nobody to move, until ordered."

It was extraordinarily quiet. The scene was isolated. No one moved. No one spoke. Georgina leaned against Bishop. She was trembling.

When the sound of the aircraft had diminished, Frisnay asked, "Craddock, what are your terms?"

"Listen carefully, please. I am getting into this car, and leaving the airport, unmolested—"

"You haven't a chance in—"

"Listen carefully. If anyone makes an attempt to stop me, I will fire the Z.69 at random. *At random.* You have some twenty men here. There are two women. There are other people beginning to gather, attracted by this spectacle. They are innocent members of the public. Inspector Frisnay, their safety is in your hands. Entirely in your hands. Do you understand?"

Frisnay found it difficult to speak. He managed. He said:

"Yes, I understand. But how far will you get?"

"As far as I wish. You understand your position, and your responsibilities. I am leaving now. Please give your orders."

Frisnay did not move.

"Craddock, you haven't a chance of getting far. It won't be worth it. You'll put your neck in a rope."

"Please give your orders."

Frisnay waited, then said, "Very well." He looked round. "Open the cordon. Let this man go through. Until he's gone, no one is to move. *No one is to move.*"

Craddock nodded.

"Thank you."

He got into the XK-120 and started the engine, turning the car neatly. His right hand never left the edge of the door. The Z.69 swept a harmless arc across the cordon. Frisnay watched, standing perfectly still. The car moved away through the gap in the cordon, and accelerated towards the main gates.

Bishop murmured, "It was all you could do, Freddie."

It was a moment before Frisnay said, "I know." He walked over to his car. "Brown, get a signal out. All divisions, action. Put a fix on Craddock's car. He's not to be stopped, but once they've picked him up, he's not to be lost. Now heading south."

ROOK'S GAMBIT

"Yes, sir." Brown hesitated. "Can't we—?"

"No. We can't. Not yet."

Bishop left Georgina's side, and came up to the G.P. car. He listened, with Frisnay, to the signal going out. When it was finished, Frisnay said to Brown, "Let's not forget to mention that Craddock has the Z.69 and is prepared to kill, wholesale."

Brown put it through. Bishop said:

"Sorry, Freddie."

"Not your fault. He's still in the country. So is the Z.69. I'm not worried that we shan't get him. I just hope it doesn't kill too many people, in the final rush." He looked round, and called, "Get back to your cars." There were people still collecting, drawn to the scene. The cordon fell away. Vic came up to the G.P.

" 'Lo, Hugo."

He touched her hand.

"I never rang you back, did I?"

She questioned him, not speaking, for a second; then she relaxed. "You're out of danger now, you crazy nut. Thank God, at least, for that." She turned away. "Where's Georgina?"

He said, "Over—" and stopped.

Vic said, "She didn't get into your car—"

"Freddie."

"Well?"

"Hutton's gone."

Frisnay said in a flat voice, "Sergeant. Find Hutton. Take six men."

"Yes, sir."

"She can't have gone far. Constable, check the Paris plane. It's leaving in fifteen minutes. Take Smith with you. Make certain she's not on board." He turned as Brown called:

"Mr. Frisnay."

"Well?"

"Call coming through, sir."

"What's the gist?"

"Car used by Craddock found abandoned, one mile from airport, south road. Search continues."

"So he's changed horses."

Bishop said, "Making back to his hotel."

"Think so?"

"There's the chance he left something vital there, that's got to be destroyed or taken with him when he leaves the country."

Frisnay said, "When he what?" His eyes looked out from recesses in solid oak carving. He got into the G.P. car. "All right, Brown. Back to base."

Bishop watched him drive away. Beside him, Vic said:

"That was difficult, for Mr. Frisnay."

"Yes. For a man like him, the easiest thing is usually difficult to do."

"Have we lost Craddock, for good?"

"I shouldn't think so." He took her arm. "I'm going to keep in touch with Freddie. Coming with me?"

"Can I?" She said it deliberately, looking up at him. He said:

"You want a re-establishment of relationships, don't you?"

"No. I want to know if you still like me."

He said, "I can't tell you, here."

"Then I'll go along with you. What did you say my most attractive characteristic was?"

"Adhesiveness."

They got into the car. She sat with her hands round her knees. "Another word for which is possessiveness."

He said, "Is it?" He backed the car deftly, swinging the long bonnet round.

She said, gazing through the windscreen as they sped discreetly through the gates, "I wonder which would be more wonderful, to know you all my life and never be really near you, or to possess you, utterly, for a little time."

He dropped the weighted lever into top, and the sedanca settled into her stride, southwards for the Metropolis. He could still see the room in her little hotel in Madrid, with the sounds of the Plaza coming in at her window on the soft dark air, the wink of light on the bottle of Vichy that had stood near the window, the sound of her breath in the quietness, the touch of the magic among ordinary things in the small high room where the notice said that the tap-water was not for drinking and that baths were instantly available, given a day's notice... the ordinary things came back almost more vividly than the magic there, because magic was fleeting, caught on the wing, and then lost in the next trembling moment, leaving the cry of a ticket-seller, dust along a shelf, a broken coat-hanger, a labelled key.

"Vic."

"Yes?"

"I hope we know each other a long time."

"And keep our independence."

"That's up to you. It's a valuable thing to lose."

She took out a cigarette. "Have you a match?"

He dug in his pocket. She touched his hand. She lit her cigarette and said:

"What do you mean, by a long time?"

"Oh, years."

She sat back nestling on the seat, drawing her legs up.

"Yes," she said in a moment. "Wonderful."

22nd MOVE

FRISNAY SAT behind his desk. He had opened a box of matches an hour before, and had piled them into a pyramid, a skyscraper, and a suspension-bridge. Now he was trying to build a Dome of Discovery. He sat there with his face carved out of *lignum vitae*. Bishop was walking up and down. He had walked, in the last hour, three miles from the filing-cabinets to the wall-map, and two miles, one thousand seven hundred and fifty-two yards from the map to the cabinets. He was going, at this moment, in that latter direction. Vic was sitting in the big leather-covered chair, compiling statistics. She judged Frisnay to have moved all the matches three times, many of them twice that number of times, and a few of them so many times that the phosphorus was wearing off. She judged that Bishop had smoked half an ounce of tobacco, wasting half that weight in dottle, and filling an equivalent of five hundred cubic feet with smoke.

Sergeant Flack had looked in four times. The telephones had rung a score of times. The clock had gone from two-fifty to three-fifty-five and she had got up twice to open the windows. Frisnay had got up once to shut them. They were open now. The sound of traffic drifted in, from Whitehall.

The inter-phone buzzer sounded. Frisnay completed the second story of his Dome of Discovery and snapped the switch down.

"Yes?"

"Miss Gorringe is here, sir."

"Show her in."

Bishop said, "Who?"

Frisnay said, "Miss Vera Gorringe, M.A. God bless her."

"Amen."

The door opened and she came in with a deft well-groomed entrance that understated her poise to perfection. Hugo took her hands. He said, "Are you all right?"

"Me? I'm fine." She had been home to change. "Did you get my message, Freddie?"

He sat down again behind his desk.

"Yes, we did. You were right. Hutton had the

Z.69. Now Craddock has it—"

"Craddock!"

"The ball," murmured Bishop, "has arrived in square two."

She said, "He took it from her?"

Frisnay said, "And walked out whistling."

She leaned elegantly against the desk. "Where is he now?"

"We're waiting to hear," Frisnay said. "There's a search on."

Bishop said, "Gorry, how did you get clear?"

She asked for a cigarette and said, "Well, the man told me he was going to perforate the nape of my neck with a burst of small-arms fire, so I turned the whole outfit over at medium speed. You know, the way you showed me."

Bishop grinned faintly. "What damage?"

"A wheel got airborne, and the roof—"

"I mean to you."

"Oh, just fallen arches; and there's something stuck in my throat. The gear-lever, I think." She looked for an ashtray, and found one, somewhere among the litter of matches. She said, "How long have you been—?"

The end telephone rang and Frisnay took it up and said:

"Yes?"

Operations said, "We've got a fix on Craddock, sir. He's gone into a hotel in Bayswater."

"That was the hotel where we first checked him?"

"Yes, sir."

Frisnay said, "Bottle him up. We're joining you. Any news of Hutton?"

"No, sir. She's vanished."

"Never mind."

He dropped the receiver and put down the switch of the inter-phone.

"Sir?"

"Flack. They've got a fix on Craddock at the Grange Hotel in Bayswater Road. Get Plan B going."

"Yes, sir."

Frisnay got up. The matches scattered. As he went out he said, "I'm going to see the Assistant Commissioner. This time I want orders to shoot to kill."

The area bounded by West Lane, Park Crescent, Daignton Gardens, and Bayswater Road was quiet. Traffic, now slowly building up to the rush-hour, had been diverted in both directions, and three side-streets were blocked. Upwards of twenty squad-cars were in attendance, placed strategically for emergency movement. The cordon on foot was some ninety men strong.

Signals were coming in on an open network.

A Post Office van was parked within fifty yards of the Grange Hotel. Its crew were jamming any short-wave radio signals that might be sent out from the hotel. The telephones were blocked and tapped.

Around the fringe of the cordon, people, coming away from work or sight-seeing from the provinces, stood about, asking questions. There were no answers. They were kept moving.

Outside the hotel, which was in a crescent driveway of gravel and shrubs, Frisnay stood talking to Bishop. Vic was near them, standing by the gray sedanca. Miss Gorringe was at the wheel, watching the front of the hotel.

"It's wonderful," Frisnay said. "We've got permission to use any means we like. Short of shooting to kill. What the hell is the use of that?"

"Have to get him some other way," Bishop said. He had never seen Frisnay so angry ever.

"That's the only way. I've talked to Veiss again. He says the Z.69 can stop every move—unless we can shoot Craddock from behind—and shoot to kill."

"Has he shown himself, at any of the windows?"

"I've had no report. He's probably burning papers, or making drawings of the Z.69, or just sitting up there with a bottle of Scotch and laughing his bloody head off." He gazed woodenly up at the hotel. "It's wonderful. We've got the phones blocked; there's a mobile unit jamming the ether; there's a full-strength cordon; we've closed five streets and set up two diversions. Craddock is where we want him—in a trap. And all he's got to do is walk out of that doorway and down those steps, and say please, and we let him through. It's wonderful."

"Just as he did at the airport."

"Just like that."

"Have they picked up Hutton?"

"No. She's only the small-fry now. We haven't got more than a routine hunt on for her. Whoever has the Z.69 is the big-fry—and the big-fry is in there." He called, "Sergeant, get those two cars closed in a bit more and face 'em the other way."

The Sergeant acknowledged. Bishop looked up at the yellow-brick Victorian façade and thought about Craddock. It was hard to get a man like Craddock, because he was the kind of man whose business was staying free. He was an expert, experienced free-lance with the freedom of action unhampered by the need for orders.

"Freddie."

"Yes?"

"Send me in."

"Not this time."

"Take a chance."

"Nothing doing. You make one attempt to go in there and I'll have you arrested and taken away. Just as protective custody."

"You're a two-faced shyster."

"If one man, going into that hotel, could do any good, I'd go in there myself."

"You can't take a gun in. I could."

"Go up those steps, Hugo, and you're in the Black Maria. Do I repeat that?"

"No. But if I took a gun in, and—"

"My men have got orders, Hugo. If they see you make a move like that, you're copped. You won't even be here to see the curtain down."

Bishop shrugged.

"Yes, Inspector."

He wandered towards his car. Vic said, "What's going to happen?"

"Ask Craddock. It's his move."

Miss Gorringe said, "How's Freddie feeling?" She said it quietly.

He leaned on the door-ledge of the car. He said, "You know when there's a straight flight of duck, and the light's behind you, and they come across in a perfect line, and you take aim, and fire, and find the thing isn't loaded?"

She said, "Is there any possible way?"

"Of getting Craddock? Yes. Shooting to kill. Shooting him in the back, when he's not ready.

Shooting him before he can squeeze that thing even for a second. He's got to be dropped as dead as a sparrow. And there are no orders to shoot." He turned his head and looked at Frisnay. Frisnay was standing alone, a little way from the nearest car. "Sometimes he must envy the methods of a trigger-conscious Chicago cop. Only sometimes, but one of the times is now."

He looked up at the hotel. There were five stories. The porch opened on to a flight of seven steps, wide stone steps that shelved graciously down to the gravel driveway. That was where Craddock would come down, in a minute from now, or an hour from now. And walk away whistling.

He turned back and said to Miss Gorringe:

"They never picked up Hutton."

"No?"

He said, "I wonder where she is."

Vic said, "She got a plane, somehow."

"Think so?" He remembered what he had told Georgina, in the car, about the sun going down towards evening. He had never thought she would listen to such a specious line, but it had been worth trying. Anything had been worth trying. He said, "I'd like to have her here."

Miss Gorringe looked at him. "Why?"

"Because she's the Red Queen. No one else can

make the sort of check we need." He scraped damp earth from his shoe, along the running-board. It fell away softly, on to the gravel. "What about trying her number, Gorry?"

"Would she be there?"

"She might be."

"It seems too easy."

"That could be a bad reason for not trying. There's a phone-box on the corner there."

She opened the door, and put one elegant shoe on the running-board. He fished up three pennies from his pocket. "You know her number?"

"Yes," Miss Gorringe said. She took the coppers and walked towards the corner, passing Frisnay, saying something to him. Bishop followed her a little way, coming up to Frisnay.

"What did she say, Freddie?"

"What?"

"Gorry."

"Oh. To keep smiling, or something. But I'm not smiling."

Bishop went on, and inched open the door of the telephone-box. Miss Gorringe was talking. She glanced at him, and gave an imperceptible nod of surprise. He didn't know whether she was talking to Georgina Hutton or someone else. He murmured:

"She there?"

Miss Gorringe nodded quickly. He kept his

voice low. "Tell her where Craddock is. This hotel."

She spoke into the phone again. In a moment she rang off, and he opened the door of the box wider for her as she came out. She was still looking surprised.

"What made you think she was there, Hugo?"

"I didn't think she was. I thought she might possibly be. Cleaning up evidence, or getting drunk, or making clay images of Craddock and spearing them with hat-pins. What did she say when you told her he was here?"

"She said, 'You're certain?' I said yes. That's all. She hung up."

They walked slowly back to where Frisnay was standing.

Bishop said, "Freddie, I've got a proposition."

"No," Frisnay said. "You try it, and you're in the Black Maria."

"I'm not asking if I can go in there. This is a different proposition."

"They're all dynamite, your propositions. I've got enough T.N.T. on my hands now. Forget it."

"Listen, Freddie; I can rope in Hutton for you."

"You can?" He didn't seem very interested.

"I know she's only the small-fry. But she's young enough to grow. I'd like to talk to her."

"So would I."

"If I could get her here, would you let her through the cordon?"

Frisnay swivelled his head slowly.

"Why?"

"Just because I'd like to talk to her."

"If you can get her here, yes, I'd let her through. But I wouldn't let her through twice. Once inside this ring, she stays."

"That would suit me. It's a deal?"

"How d'you think you can find her?"

"It's a deal?"

Frisnay said, "Yes."

Bishop looked across at Sergeant Flack. Frisnay called him over. "If Hutton shows up, she's to be let through the cordon and told where Mr. Bishop is."

"Yes, sir."

Flack went away to put the order out. Bishop prodded the ash down in his *meerschaum*, and gazed up at the yellow-brick façade.

The rush-hour was nearing peak. From inside the quiet cordon they could hear the sound of the traffic swelling, eastwards in the streets. The light was fading, very slowly. It would not be dusk, yet, for an hour, but surfaces were losing their sheen, and angles were blurring, minute by minute as the vigil went on.

A signal came through to the G.P. car, at ten to six. Brown said to Frisnay, "We've got permission to go in with tear-gas, sir, at your discretion. There's a delivery on its way."

Frisnay grunted. "Meet it, and get it distributed to the active sections."

Bishop said, "Are you going to use it?"

"At this stage, we might as well go in there throwing peanuts about; but there might be a chance, later." His head lifted suddenly.

Bishop said, "Freddie."

"Yes."

Many of the men were looking towards Frisnay, waiting for orders. Others were still watching the porch of the hotel. Craddock stood there for a few seconds, and then slowly came down the steps. He was carrying a brief-case, in his left hand. The Z.69 was in his right.

Bishop checked his watch. There had been time. It could work. He looked up again. Craddock stood on the lowest step, his head turning slowly as if he were counting the men who were assembled here. His voice came:

"Inspector Frisnay."

Frisnay said to Flack, "No one to move. That's important." He called clearly, "I'm here, Major Craddock."

Craddock's face was pale. He looked a tired man. He stood with his feet together, his body rigid, twelve yards or less from Frisnay's car.

"You're wasting your time again. The situation remains the same, and under my control." He spoke with careful authority.

A man moved. The gravel crunched under his foot. Frisnay turned his head. The man had shifted his feet, nothing more. Frisnay looked back at Craddock. If anyone went forward, to try nailing Craddock, he'd do more than break orders. He'd kill himself.

Craddock was looking about him, turning his head slowly. Bishop thought of an eagle, released from a cage, studying its way to freedom before it rose.

His head stopped turning. It had turned back to face Frisnay.

"I'm leaving here now. Until I reach the Continent I shall take care to keep in crowded places all the time. I shall go by train, to Dover, for that reason. I know you'll remember your duty is to the public, and that their lives are in your hands."

Miss Gorringe, standing beside the gray sedanca, murmured:

"Hugo."

"Yes. I've seen her."

They watched. She was standing between two of the cars that were drawn up near the hotel steps. She wore the same apple-green suit, with the striped scarf. Her face, like Craddock's, was strained. She came a few paces towards him, but he moved his right hand and she stopped.

She said in a moment, "You're taking me with you, Charles."

He said nothing.

Bishop didn't want to watch, any more. He had arranged this, but he didn't want to see it go through. But it was impossible not to watch.

"I can't stay here now." Her voice sounded thin, in the quiet air. "I helped you to get the Z.69. I can help you to take it home."

An odd word, Bishop thought. Home.

Craddock was still looking at her. He said, "One can travel more easily than two. I'm sorry." He turned his head. "Mr. Frisnay, please give orders to let me through your men."

"There'll be no orders."

"I must warn you again that—"

"Craddock." She said it through her teeth. She had moved another step forward and the travel-coat swung, draped over her arm. Craddock turned quickly and she stopped. Her face went white. "They can't stop you going. But you'll take me with you."

"You are out of your mind." He looked upwards. Along the edge of the roof, above him and to his right, a line of starlings were perched. "Mr. Frisnay, please attend." He moved the Z.69.

A faint murmur came from the people watching. As it died, there came the soft thudding of the birds against the gravel. They lay still. Craddock looked down at them.

"Mr. Frisnay, the first man to move will be the death of a dozen."

He stepped on to the gravel driveway.

Georgina said, "You'll take me with you."

Craddock, perhaps hearing something in her voice, turned his head. He saw the gun in her hand. There was surprise on his face. He had thought of everything, almost everything. The Z.69 made no sound; there was no flash. The sound of the gun was rough and staccato. She put five shots into him before she dropped. She dropped with the sudden thud of a dead-weight, as the birds had done.

The silence was frozen. Vic murmured, "Hugo, are they both—"

"Yes. It sometimes happens, in a duel."

Frisnay had gone forward. He picked up the Z.69. Bishop said, "It was the Red Queen's move, and that is checkmate."

He watched Vic walking across to the telephone-box.

Miss Gorringe steadied her voice. "Where's she going, Hugo?"

He said, "To scoop the street."

Adam Hall is the pseudonym of Elleston Trevor, the author of over 20 novels. Mr. Trevor resides in Cave Creek, Arizona.